VISITORS

FROM

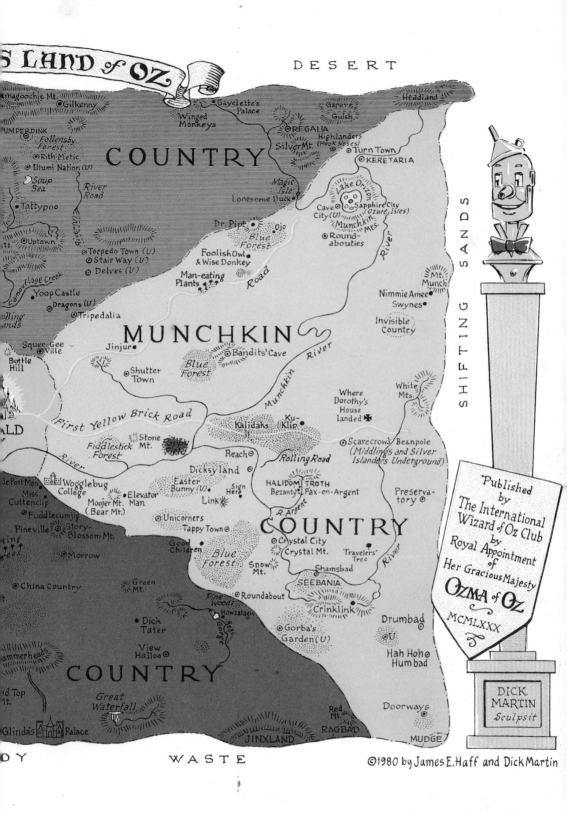

DESERT

S LAND of OZ

amagoochie Mt.
Gilkenny
Gayelette's Palace
Winged Monkeys
Gapers Gulch
Headland

UMPERDINK
Follensby Forest
Rith Metic
Illumi Nation (U)
Soup Sea
Tattypoo

COUNTRY
REGALIA
SilverMt.
Highlanders (Hook Noses)
Turn Town
KERETARIA

River Road
Magic Isle
Lonesome Duck
Lake Orizon
Cave City (U)
Sapphire City (Ozure Isles)
Munchkin Mts.

Uptown
Dr. Pipt
Ojo
Blue Forest
Round-abouties

Torpedo Town (U)
Stair Way (U)
Delves (U)
Foolish Owl & Wise Donkey
Man-eating Plants
Road
Mt. Munch

Camouflage Creek
Yoop Castle
Dragons (U)
Tripedalia
Nimmie Amee
Swynes

olling ands
MUNCHKIN
Jinjur
Bandits' Cave
Munchkin River
Invisible Country

Squee-Gee Ville
Bottle Hill
Shutter Town
Blue Forest
White Mts.

ALD
First Yellow Brick Road
Stone Mt.
Poppy Field
Where Dorothy's House landed
Scarecrow's Beanpole (Middlings and Silver Islanders Underground)

River
Fiddlestick Forest
Reach
Kalidahs
Ku-Klip
Rolling Road

de fost Man
Wogglebug College
Dicksyland
Easter Bunny (U)
Sign Here
HALIDOM TROTH
Bezanty Pax-on-Argent
Preserva-tory

Miss. Cuttenclip
Elevator Man
Moojer Mt. (Bear Mt.)
Link
R. Argent

Fuddlecumjig
Pineville
Story-Blossom Mt.
Unicorners
Tappy Town
COUNTRY
River

ting rees
Morrow
Good Children
Blue Forest
Crystal City
Crystal Mt.
Snow Mt.
Travelers' Tree

China Country
Green Mt.
Shamsbad
SEEBANIA

Pine Woods
Roundabout
Crinklink
Drumbad

ammerheads
Dick Tater
Howzatagin
Gorba's Garden (U)
U
Hah Hoh Humbad

COUNTRY
View Halloo
Great Waterfall
Red Mt.
Doorways

d Top t.
Glinda's Palace
JINXLAND
RAGBAD
MUDGE

DY
WASTE
©1980 by James E. Haff and Dick Martin

SHIFTING SANDS

Published by The International Wizard of Oz Club by Royal Appointment of Her Gracious Majesty OZMA of OZ MCMLXXX

DICK MARTIN Sculpsit

THE FOURTEEN OZ BOOKS WRITTEN BY

L. FRANK BAUM, THE ROYAL HISTORIAN OF OZ

L. Frank Baum, the Royal Historian of Oz

VISITORS

FROM

The Wild Adventures of Dorothy,
the Scarecrow, and the Tin Woodman

MARTIN GARDNER

ST. MARTIN'S PRESS

New York

Production Editor: David Stanford Burr
Design by Abby Kagan

Library of Congress Cataloging-in-Publication Data

Gardner, Martin.
    Visitors from Oz / Martin Gardner.
      p. cm.
    Sequel to: The wizard of Oz by L. Frank Baum.
    ISBN 0-312-19353-X
    I. Baum, L. Frank (Lyman Frank), 1856–1919. Wizard of Oz.
    II. Title.
    PS3557.A714V57   1998
    813'.54—dc21   98-21114
                                                  CIP

First U.S. Edition: November 1998

10 9 8 7 6 5 4 3 2 1

TO FRED MEYER,

who as longtime secretary of the
International Wizard of Oz Club, did so much to
increase the recognition of L. Frank Baum
as our nation's greatest writer of fantasy for children.

Never question the truth of
what you fail to understand, for the
world is full of wonders.
—*the white pearl in L. Frank Baum's* Rinkitink in Oz

They [fairy tales] make rivers run
with wine only to make us remember,
for one wild moment,
that they run with water.
—*G. K. Chesterton, in* Orthodoxy, *Chapter 4*

CONTENTS

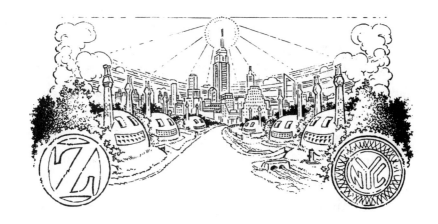

PREFACE

IT IS sad that so many children and adults today know about Oz only because they have seen the MGM movie that starred Judy Garland. *The Wonderful Wizard of Oz*, on which that musical was based, was Lyman Frank Baum's first Oz book. He wrote thirteen others. In my opinion many of his later Oz books, as well as some of his non-Oz fantasies, are better written and more entertaining than *The Wizard*.

After Baum died in 1919, Ruth Plumly Thompson wrote even more Oz books than he did. John R. Neill, who illustrated all of Baum's and Thompson's Oz books except *The Wizard*, wrote three Oz books. Jack Snow, author of *Who's*

Who in Oz (1954), tried his hand on two Oz books. Others have since been written by still later authors.

I loved Baum's Oz books as a child, and am proud to say that I wrote the first article that went into detail about Baum's colorful life. Titled "The Royal Historian of Oz," it first ran as a two-part article in *Fantasy and Science Fiction* (January and February 1955), and has most recently been reprinted in *The Night Is Large,* a collection of essays published in 1996 by St. Martin's Press. I have also provided introductions to five Dover paperback reprints of books by Baum. You will find my appreciation of *The Tin Woodman of Oz* in the fall 1996 issue of *The Baum Bugle.*

The Baum Bugle is the official magazine of The International Wizard of Oz Club, founded in 1957 by Justin Schiller when he was in his early teens. Justin is now the nation's top dealer in rare books for children. On the masthead of his first mimeographed issues of *The Baum Bugle* I am listed as Chairman of the Board of Directors! Today this quarterly is a handsome periodical, featuring scholarly articles and pictures in full color. You can subscribe by joining the club: P.O. Box 266, Kalamazoo, MI 49004-0266.

The first book-length biography of Baum, *To Please a Child* (1961) was written by Russell P. MacFall when he was night editor of the *Chicago Tribune. L. Frank Baum: Royal Historian of Oz,* by Angelica Shirley Carpenter and Jean Shirley, was published in 1992. These books will soon be superseded by Michael Patrick Hearn's definitive biography on which he has been working for more than a decade. Hearn is the author, among other books, of *The Annotated Wizard of Oz* (1973), and editor of a 1983 anthology of critical essays about Baum's work.

Raylyn Moore's study of Baum's writings, *Wonderful Wizard, Marvelous Land,* was published in 1974 with a preface by Ray Bradbury. Michael Riley's *Oz and Beyond: The Fantasy World of L. Frank Baum,* appeared in 1997. Four large, lavishly illustrated picture books also testify to the growing recognition of Baum's achievement: *The Wizard of Oz,* the official 50th Anniversary pictorial history (a history of the MGM film) by John Fricke, Jay Scarfone, and William Stillman (1989); *The World of Oz* by Allen Eyles (1985); *The Oz Scrapbook* by David L. Greene and Dick Martin (1977); and *The Wizard of Oz Collector's Treasury,* by Jay Scarfone and William Stillman (1992). It would take several pages just to list the essays about Baum that have appeared in various periodicals. Gore Vidal's lengthy review of a reprinting of all of Baum's Oz books that first ran in *The New York Review of Books,* and can be found in his 1993 collection, *United States: Essays, 1952–1992.*

All my life I have hesitated about writing another Oz book. I never much cared for novels and short stories featuring Sherlock Holmes that were written by authors other than Conan Doyle. Somehow they never seemed to portray the "real" Holmes and Watson. My respect for Baum's "canon" was similarly so great that I felt it was a kind of sacrilege to write an Oz book that was not about the "real" Oz.

As the centennial anniversary of the publication of *The Wizard* in the year 2000 approaches, I have finally persuaded myself that it is impossible to damage the Royal Historian's reputation by perpetrating a new Oz book. I have done my best to come close to Baum's simple style, and to be faithful to the whimsical land and characters he created. Like Baum,

I cannot decide whether this book is solely for youngsters, or also for older readers who are still young at heart.

—Martin Gardner

Hendersonville, North Carolina

January 1998

VISITORS FROM

Oz

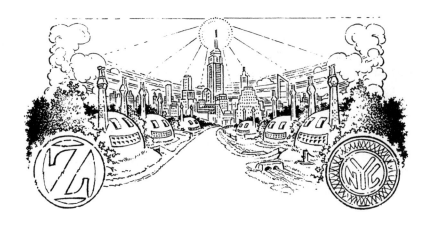

1

——◦◦◦——

SAMUEL GOLD

"YOU HAVE a dreamy look on your face," said Mrs. Samuel Gold to her husband. He was seated opposite her at the breakfast table. "Is something troubling you?"

"No," replied Sammy. "I was just thinking about the new Oz film I'm planning to produce."

"I sometimes think you think too much about Oz," said Gloria Gold. "The Oz books must have made a strong impression on you when you were a boy."

"They did indeed. You know, I learned to read by looking over my mother's shoulder while she read aloud *The Wizard of Oz*. It was very embarrassing in first grade. The teacher was doing her best to teach everyone in the class how to read.

I was bored to death. She even asked me to keep quiet when she held up placards with simple words like *cat* and *dog*. I was always the first to call out the names."

"You had such great success with your *Alice in Carrolland*," said Gloria. "Have you decided yet on which Oz book to dramatize?"

"I have. It will be L. Frank Baum's sixth Oz book.

"And what book is that?"

"The Emerald City of Oz."

If you have read Baum's later Oz books you may recall the amusing plot of *The Emerald City*. The wicked Nome King assembles hordes of evil creatures to assist his army of Nomes in a plan to invade Oz and overthrow its ruler, the beautiful Princess Ozma. The Nomes dig a long tunnel from their home in the adjacent land of Ev—a tunnel that goes under the Deadly Desert. Any living creature touching the sand of this dreadful desert turns instantly to dust.

The Nome King's fiendish plan is to emerge from the tunnel at a spot near Ozma's palace and quickly seize control of the throne. It would be, he was certain, an easy conquest. He knew the palace would be guarded only by a harmless old gentleman called the Soldier with the Green Whiskers.

Oz fans will remember how the Scarecrow, using the excellent brains given to him by the Wizard, thinks of a clever scheme to foil the invaders. He asks Ozma to use the powers of her Magic Belt to cause the tunnel to fill with thick dust. The dust makes the invaders so thirsty that when they emerge from the tunnel they rush to drink from the nearby Forbidden Fountain. It is called Forbidden because no one in Oz is allowed to drink from it. When the evil soldiers imbibe its sparkling Water of Oblivion they instantly forget who they are and what they came to do. The invasion of course collapses. The Nome King, now behaving like a baby, and his equally bewildered cohorts are all sent back to Ev.

Samuel Gold was Hollywood's wealthiest, most famous producer of blockbuster motion pictures. He had scored a triumphant hit with his animated version of Lewis Carroll's two books about Alice, using computer graphics instead of hand-drawn art. The film had earned Gold Pictures hundreds of millions of dollars. Now he had decided to follow it with an even more ambitious musical—a computer-animated version of *The Emerald City of Oz*. The year 2000 would be the hundred-year anniversary of Baum's first Oz book. What could be a better time, Sammy reasoned, to release a new and spectacular Oz film?

It was a sultry summer morning in Hollywood when Gold entered his sumptuously furnished studio office, but inside the air was fresh and cool. Sammy was a trifle plump, with pale blue eyes and long, wavy blond hair that almost touched his shoulders. Although he had recently turned thirty-seven, his round, boyish face made him look much younger.

"There was great publicity for my Alice film," Gold said to his secretary. She was seated by his desk, her pencil poised over a notebook to take dictation. "I sent my star, the girl who played Alice, on the rounds of every major talk show. Along with her went actors dressed to look like the Mad Hatter, the Ugly Duchess, and other characters in the *Alice* books. They were big hits with the television audience."

"As I recall," said the secretary, "didn't that movie set all attendance records for the past thirty years?"

"It did, it did," said Gold, leaning back in a red leather chair, his chubby hands clasped behind his head. "What can

I do to publicize my Oz film? Sending whoever plays Dorothy around the country to be a guest on radio and TV shows is no problem. But I can't dress up actors to resemble such characters as the Scarecrow and the Tin Woodman. They wouldn't look anything like the film's computer graphics. Are you familiar with Baum's Oz books?"

The secretary shook her head. "All I know about Oz is what I learned from the Judy Garland movie."

"A great pity," said Gold. "You would have loved the Oz books when you were a little girl. I intend to base my graphics on the color pictures by John R. Neill, the Royal Illustrator of Oz. He learned from Baum exactly what everyone in Oz looked like."

Sammy Gold was one of those rare Oz enthusiasts who actually believed Oz is real. Although almost all Oz fans take for granted that Oz is a mythical fairyland which flourished only in the vivid imagination of Baum, Oz's Royal Historian, Gold was a true believer. By the time he was ten, he had eagerly read every Oz book by Baum and most of the later Oz books by Baum's worthy successor Ruth Plumly Thompson, and by Jack Snow and others. He loved every Oz book. He knew all their plots by heart.

Young Sammy's parents were sure he was just pretending when he talked as if Oz were as real as Kansas. Oz buffs who listened to his speeches at annual conventions of the International Wizard of Oz Club suspected he was only pretending to believe, the way Sherlock Holmes fans pretend Holmes and Watson were actual persons. Or perhaps Gold was a trifle mad?

Even Gloria assumed her husband was putting her on when he talked about Oz. But Sammy didn't care what others thought. He *knew* Oz was not just a made-up country. When he saw the MGM film with Judy Garland he was furious with the way it ended. How *dare* they turn Baum's faithful reporting into something as trivial as a dream!

While Gold was leaning back in his chair, gazing at a large framed map of Oz on a wall near him, an idea suddenly struck him like a thunderbolt. He leaped to his feet and shouted "Eureka!" The secretary was so startled that she dropped her pencil on the floor.

A gray cat—Sammy had named her Eureka after Dorothy's white cat—stood up in a far corner of the office, yawned, stretched her legs, then strolled slowly over to rub her side against Gold's calf.

"No, no, Eureka," Gold said as he stroked the cat. "I wasn't calling you. Don't you know that *eureka* is an ancient Greek exclamation meaning 'I have had found it.'?"

Eureka purred and looked as if she understood, but didn't say anything. Animals outside Oz can listen and even think dimly, but are unable to speak.

What great notion had exploded in Sammy's brain? It had occurred to him that it might be possible, just barely possible, to persuade Dorothy to return to America for a brief visit! Maybe she could bring along the Scarecrow and the tin man! As all Oz buffs know, in *The Emerald City of Oz* Princess Ozma granted Dorothy's wish to become a permanent resident of Oz. Using her Magic Belt, Ozma then teleported Uncle Henry and Aunt Em to the Emerald City where they could be with their niece and live comfortably forever.

If Dorothy and her two friends would be willing to come to the United States, Gold wondered, would they also agree to appear on television and radio talk shows to speak about the film he was planning? It would be fantastic publicity!

Gold had a formidable competitor. He was Buffalo Odersby Boggs, founder and president of Boggs Pictures.

Boggs was a tall, muscular man, totally bald, with shifty black eyes and a bushy black mustache. He always looked as if he needed a shave. When he wasn't around, his employees called him B.O. because he so seldom bathed. He had been married only once. His wife quickly divorced him after she found she couldn't persuade him to bathe more often than every two weeks.

An anoymous bit of verse that once circulated secretly among Boggs's screenwriters went as follows:

Buffalo Boggs, it is said,
One summer lay down on his bed.
He stuck his bare feet through a window.
Next morning the neighbors were dead!

Boggs had a reputation in Hollywood as a man who would go to any lengths, fair or foul, to discredit or even injure a rival. Rumors were that he had close ties to New York City mobsters who had assisted him financially in building his film empire.

Like Gold, Boggs had announced to the world that he too was planning to use computer graphics for a new musical fantasy. It was to be a film based on J. M. Barrie's classic play about Peter Pan. A contract had already been signed by Madonna to take the title role.

Gold rubbed his hands and chuckled to himself while he imagined how angry and jealous Boggs would be if Dorothy and her pals came to the United States to chat about his forthcoming film.

"Who cares about Peter and Wendy?" Gold said to himself. "After all, Neverland is pure fantasy. It never, *never* was a real place like Oz."

The best person in Oz to contact, Gold decided, was Glinda. This red-haired good witch was the most powerful sorceress in Oz or anywhere else. He knew from Baum's Royal History that Glinda kept in touch with every event in Oz by reading about them daily in her Magic Book of Records. Did she also keep in touch with events on Earth?

Telephones long ago had become commonplace in Oz. Almost every household had one. Would the good citizens of Oz soon be demanding television sets, refrigerators, washing machines, cars, and airplanes? Would they want home computers? Was it possible that Glinda already owned a computer and had tapped into the Internet?

If you have read *The Emerald City of Oz*, you will recall how decades ago Glinda decided that too many persons from the outside world were finding their way to Oz. The list included the Wizard, who floated there in a balloon from Omaha, Betsy Bobbin from Oklahoma, Trot and Cap'n Bill from California, Shaggy Man and his brother from Colorado, Button-Bright from Philadelphia, and of course Dorothy Gale from Kansas. So Glinda made an irrevocable decision. She cut Oz permanently off from the Earth by making it completely invisible to outsiders.

How did Glinda accomplish this monumental feat? It was by transporting Oz and its surrounding enchanted countries to a parallel universe very close to Earth but separated from earth by a short distance through a space of four dimensions.

Imagine a vast number of almost identical universes side by side like the pages of a book. Flat creatures living on one page would be unaware of an adjacent page even though it was only a hair's distance away in a direction they could not comprehend. In a similar fashion we live in a space of three dimensions. Another universe is directly above us, separated from us by only a few feet of four-dimensional space. Using powerful sorcery, Glinda lifted Oz from our universe, moving it several feet through the fourth dimension, to the next parallel universe. Oz came to rest on a previously uninhabited Earth almost exactly like ours, with its own sun, moon, and distant stars.

If Glinda was on the Internet, Gold speculated, she may have joined several hundred Oz fans who were on-line as a group called the Ozmapolitans. Of course she would be using a fictitious name.

Gold had been one of the first to affiliate with the Ozmapolitans. To each member he sent a message asking Glinda, if she was on-line, to contact him as soon as possible. Oz fans who read his request took it to be another of what they believed was one of Sammy's jokes. They were used to him pretending that Oz was a real place.

Several days went by with no response. Then one morning Gold's computer tapped out a posting straight from Oz! Glinda had received his inquiry! Why, she wanted to know, was he trying to reach her? She added her E-mail address, using a magic charm to prevent anyone except Gold from receiving it.

Sammy was overjoyed. He told no one about Glinda's message, not even his wife, Gloria, or their two boys. The boys were spending the summer at Camp Mishawaka, in northern Minnesota. They loved the Oz books, but like their mother they refused to take their father seriously when he talked as if Oz were real.

Here is the letter Gold sent:

Dear Glinda:

I have loved and admired you ever since I read about you in L. Frank Baum's Royal History of Oz.

I am a respected producer of motion pictures. Recently I had great success with a movie based on Lewis Carroll's Alice in Wonderland *and* Through the Looking-Glass. *It has been many years since Judy Garland played a singing Dorothy in MGM's* Wizard of Oz. *I am now planning to produce a similar musical based on Baum's* Emerald City of Oz. *It's my favorite Oz book. Actors will be used to play Dorothy and Ozma, and other flesh and blood persons, but computer techniques will be required to make such characters as the Scarecrow and Tin Woodman seem as real as photographs.*

Would it be possible for you and Ozma to arrange for Dorothy, and anyone else who would care to come with her, to visit Earth for a brief period? Dorothy would not have to do anything except allow her picture to be taken and to be interviewed by reporters. I would also hope she would be willing to appear on radio and television talk shows.

Surely Dorothy would welcome a return visit to Kansas. Perhaps her friends the Scarecrow and tin man would enjoy seeing for the first time what cities here are like.

I eagerly await hearing from you.

With unbounded respect,
Samuel Gold

Glinda's lovely face was grave while she read Gold's surprising message. Since she had moved Oz to another universe it was almost as impossible for anyone to leave Oz as it was for an outsider to enter that enchanted land.

"I must phone Ozma at once," Glinda said to Mary Ann, a maidservant then engaged in dusting Glinda's ruby throne. "I can't imagine what she and Dorothy will think of Mr. Gold's ambitious plan. It certainly is an unusual request. On the other hand, as Mr. Gold suggests, Dorothy might enjoy seeing that dreary farm where she grew up."

"I should think so," replied Mary Ann. "And the Scarecrow and the Tin Woodman may well be curious about the land where their friend and rescuer once lived."

Glinda nodded. "I suppose you're right, Mary Ann. It's hard, though, to understand why any former Earthling now living here would want to go back to that violent, war-torn, unhappy globe where everyone gets sick or injured and eventually dies."

Mary Ann handed Glinda her portable phone. She pushed the buttons for Ozma's unlisted number and after a few rings Ozma answered. The Princess and Ruler of Oz listened carefully while Glinda explained who Mr. Gold was and told her about his invitation.

"I'll speak to Dorothy about it tomorrow," Ozma said. "I have no idea how she'll react. Besides, I'm not sure there's any way to get a person in Oz safely down on Earth. As you know, my Magic Belt still works inside Oz and its surrounding lands, and it can still teleport persons and things here and there on Earth. But it no longer can move persons and objects back and forth between the two universes."

"You can blame me for that, Ozma. When I managed to

move Oz to another universe—and I assure you it was no easy feat—I made certain it no longer would be possible for your Magic Belt or my powers of sorcery to teleport anyone or anything from Oz to Earth or from Earth to Oz. I often wonder if it was a wise decision. In any case, there's nothing I can do now to alter that decision."

"Will you inform Mr. Gold that there's no way we can grant his request?"

"Not just yet. There could be a way to get someone to the earth by using natural laws. We must ask Professor Woggle-bug. If anyone can devise such a way, the professor can."

Ozma ended her side of the conversation by asking, "How's the Quadling weather down there this morning?"

Quadling, of course, is one of the four regions that surround the Emerald City. On the west is the Winkie region where the dominant color is yellow. On the east is Munchkin land where the color is blue. The red Quadling country is south, and the purple Gillikin region is north.

"The weather here is beautiful as usual," Glinda replied. "We had a brief summer shower yesterday afternoon. But the sun came out, as it always does. There was a gorgeous rainbow, so I had a pleasant visit with Polychrome."

Polychrome is the dancing daughter of the Rainbow, one of the many cloud fairies in Oz.

"Give my love to Dorothy," Glinda added. "Good-bye. Let me know what Dorothy decides, and whether Professor Wogglebug can find a way to get her to Earth and back."

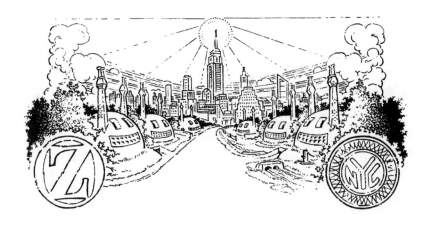

2

OZMA CALLS
A CONFERENCE

RATHER THAN consult individually with a small group of her dearest friends, Princess Ozma decided to bring them all together for a meeting to see what they thought about Samuel Gold's daring invitation. Seated around a large circular table in what Ozma called her Green Room were the following distinguished citizens of the Emerald City: Dorothy, the Scarecrow, the Tin Woodman, the Cowardly Lion, the Hungry Tiger, Toto, Betsy Bobbin, Button-Bright, and Trot.

"Yes, Ozma," said Dorothy. "I really *would* love to see Kansas again. Maybe Mr. Gold will let me fly to San Francisco to visit my cousin Zeb. Remember Zeb? After the great San Francisco earthquake of 1906 dropped both of us and the Wiz-

6.02×10²³

ard into lands below the earth's surface, you finally rescued us by teleporting us to Oz with your Magic Belt."

"I remember Zeb well," said Ozma, "and his old horse Jim. I'm sorry he and Jim decided not to remain in Oz. Have you forgotten, though, that although none of us here grow older unless we want to, this doesn't apply to those on Earth? Your cousin Zeb surely is no longer living. He would be older than a hundred by now."

"You're right, Ozma," Dorothy said with a wistful faraway look in her blue eyes. "I should have remembered how fast people on Earth grow old."

Trot shook her head when Ozma asked if she cared to accompany Dorothy. "I have no desire to see California again. My parents are long gone, I had no brothers or sisters. Besides, something could go wrong while we were on Earth and we might not be able to get back. Dorothy is much braver than I am. I don't want to risk it."

Betsy Bobbin felt the same way. "When I grew up in Tulsa it was a small village. Everybody knew everybody else. Now it's a big city with too many cars and too much crime. I'll stay here with friend Trot."

Ozma turned to Button-Bright, the little boy who was always getting lost. "Would you like to go along with Dorothy and perhaps see Philadelphia again?"

"Nope," said Button-Bright.

The Cowardly Lion and the Hungry Tiger shook their huge heads vigorously. "We wouldn't be able to talk outside Oz," said the lion. "The police would try to capture us and lock us up in some awful zoo. After all, on Earth we're considered ferocious beasts. No thanks. We'd rather stay here where we're loved and respected, and no one is afraid of us."

"Or think that I'd eat one of their precious babies," said the Hungry Tiger. He paused, then added, "Much as I would like to."

"I prefer to stay here, too," said Toto, who was able to speak as soon as he entered Oz. "It wouldn't be much fun not being able to talk to other dogs."

Ozma asked the Scarecrow for his decision.

"Yes, Your Highness. I would *very* much like to see what the United States is like. Of course everyone there will consider me a freak, but I think I'll be able to handle it. After all, they can't do much harm to a man made of cloth and straw."

"I feel the same as my friend," said the tin man. "I've read a great deal about the outside world in the books we have in our Winkie Free Library." (The Tin Woodman had for many decades ruled the Winkie region of Oz as its emperor.) "I'd love to visit the United States. And if any persons try to harm Dorothy I'll fight them off with my trusty axe."

The tin man lifted his axe and waved it through the air. Once he had been a flesh-and-blood Munchkin with the name of Nick Chopper. A wicked witch had enchanted his axe, causing it to keep slicing off parts of his body. As he lost each part, including even his head, the master tinsmith Ku-Klip, using magic glue, replaced each part with tin until Nick Chopper was made entirely of tin. Inside his hollow body was a red silk heart, stuffed with sawdust. The Wizard had given it to him at the same time he put bran in the Scarecrow's head to serve as brains, and fed the Cowardly Lion a bottle of courage.

"Thank you for your opinions," said Ozma. "Of course I'll respect all your decisions. I'll ask Glinda to inform Mr. Gold that Dorothy, along with Scarecrow and the tin man, will be visiting him as soon as we find a way, assuming we can, of sending them to Earth."

"You mentioned a moment ago," said the Scarecrow, "that Glinda recommended seeing Professor Wogglebug about how to get to Earth. As president of the College of Arts and Athletic Perfection he's one of the smartest and best informed persons in Oz. If anyone can figure out a way to get from Oz to Earth, using science instead of sorcery, and get them back safely, surely the wogglebug can. I make a motion I be allowed to call on the professor for advice."

"An excellent proposal, Scarecrow," said Ozma. "All in favor please raise your right hand."

"Or your front right paw," she added quickly, with a glance and a smile toward the lion, the tiger, and Toto.

Everyone at the table voted yes.

As you may know, Professor Wogglebug was once an ordinary tiny bug. As the Royal Historian reveals in *The Marvelous Land of Oz,* the bug hid in the warm hearth of a school where Professor Nowitall taught. To show his students what a wogglebug looked like, he put the bug in a projector and threw his image on a large screen.

A girl in the class was so frightened by the image that she tumbled off the windowsill where she had been sitting. The wogglebug took advantage of the confusion to step down from the screen in his greatly magnified state. After escaping from the school and being fitted with fine clothes, he adopted the name of H. M. Wogglebug T. E. The H. M. stood for Highly Magnified, and T. E. for Thoroughly Educated. For three years he had listened so carefully to Nowitall's lectures that he became as smart as his teacher.

Later Professor Wogglebug founded on the outskirts of the Emerald City his popular College of Arts and Athletic Perfection. Students were fond of the college because they were able to master any subject instantly by swallowing an appropriate pill. These amazing School Pills, as they were called, had been invented by the Wizard. No longer was it necessary for students to waste time reading textbooks and listening to dull lectures. To learn algebra, for example, all they had to do was take an algebra pill. The pills allowed them to spend all their time on college sports, such as football, baseball, basketball, and gymnastics.

The Scarecrow phoned Professor Wogglebug and arranged for a visit.

"It was most perceptive of you to seek my expert assistance," said the pompous wogglebug as he welcomed the Scarecrow into his cluttered office. "The task of moving from one universe to a parallel one is an intriguing problem in four-dimensional non-Euclidian geometry and the topology of space-time. But first I must inform myself about such technical matters."

The professor stood up on his long thin legs and walked over to a cupboard where he kept his learning pills. From a high shelf he selected a small bottle labeled TOPOLOGY. The pills were bright orange. He popped one into his wide mouth and washed it down with a gulp of water. For a few seconds he closed his huge insect eyes and remained silent. Suddenly he opened his eyes and recited:

"Every map on a plane or on the surface of a sphere can be colored with four colors or less so that no two adjacent regions share the same color."

"Very interesting," said the Scarecrow, "but that's no help in solving our problem."

"Quite right," replied the wogglebug. "Your observation is thoroughly justified." He closed his eyes once more for several minutes before speaking again.

"The most efficient way to get from Oz to the United States and back again is by way of a Klein Bottle."

"Pardon?" said the Scarecrow. "What, may I ask, is a Klein Bottle?"

The wogglebug opened a desk drawer from which he removed a sheet of paper and a pair of scissors. He cut a strip of paper about an inch wide and eleven inches long, gave it a half-twist, then fastened the ends together with a piece of tape.

"This," he said, holding up the paper ring, "is a topological curiosity called a Moebius band. Inspect it closely. You will perceive that it has only one side and one edge."

Topology, as the wogglebug knew, studies the properties of a structure that never change no matter how the object is stretched, twisted, or distorted. Imagine that a Moebius band is made from a rubber sheet. No matter how it is distorted, it will always have one side and one edge.

The Scarecrow took the paper model in one hand. With his other hand he moved the tip of a cloth finger all the way around the model, then around it a second time. His finger touched every spot on both of what seemed to be two sides of the band. It was hard to believe. Sure enough, the thing had only one side!

The Scarecrow then traced the band's edge twice around the model until his finger came back to where it started.

There was just one edge, not two, as Professor Wogglebug had assured him.

"Amazing!" the straw man exclaimed.

"What is even more counterintuitive," said the wogglebug, "is this. If you endeavor to cut the strip in half down its middle, you'll find it can't be done."

Professor Wogglebug took another swallow of water, then put one hand on his chest and recited:

> *A mathematician confided*
> *That a Moebius strip is one-sided.*
> *You'll get quite a laugh*
> *If you cut it in half,*
> *For it stays in one piece when divided.*

The bug handed the scissors to the Scarecrow. The insect was right again. When the band was cut down the middle, all the way around, instead of making two strips, as one would expect, it opened up into one large band twice the size of the original!

"If you initiate the cut a third of the way from one edge," said Professor Wogglebug, "the result is even more astonishing. You get one large band with a smaller one linked through it."

"I'll take your word for it," said the straw man. "But what does this ridiculous thing have to do with what you call a Klein Bottle?"

"That's more difficult to understand unless you imbibe one of my topology pills. I'll do my best to elucidate. If you take a Moebius band made with a left-handed twist, and another band made with a right-handed twist, they will be enantio-morphs of each other."

"Come again?" said the straw man. "What in the world are enantiomorphs?"

"They are mirror images, like your left and right hands or your left and right ears. Now, if you join the edges of two mirror-image Moebius bands it makes what topologists call a Klein Bottle.

Professor Wogglebug put a hand on his chest once more and recited another limerick that the topology pill had taught him:

> *A mathematician named Klein*
> *Thought the Moebius band was divine.*
>   *Said he, "If you glue*
>   *The edges of two,*
> *You'll get a weird bottle like mine."*

"A Klein Bottle," the bug continued, "is a surface devoid of edges, like the surface of a sphere. A sphere divides space into two regions, one inside, and one outside. But the Klein Bottle, like a Moebius band, has only one side. There *is* no outside or inside. An ant on what seems to be the bottle's outside can crawl to what looks like an inside without crossing an edge because the bottle *has* no edges. Here, let me draw you a picture.

The bug put on his reading glasses and sketched the picture of the Klein Bottle shown on the following page.

"Observe," he said, "that the bottle's tube passes through the bottle's surface. That's because you can't make a perfect model of a Klein Bottle in three-dimensional space. A true Klein Bottle does not intersect itself."

Professor Wogglebug's
sketch of a Klein Bottle

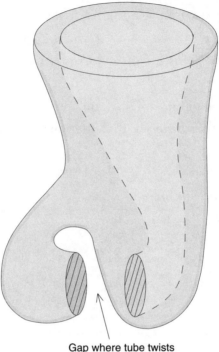

Gap where tube twists
through fourth dimension

The Scarecrow scratched his head as best he could with his padded fingers. "I'm afraid my brains, excellent though they are, aren't good enough to understand what you're saying."

"You don't need topologize," said the wogglebug, who was fond of puns. "The point to remember is this. If you construct a true Klein Bottle its tube will twist out of our space into the fourth dimension, then twist back again to enter our space on the other side of the surface. Any object dropped into the bottle will fall out of the tube because, in the fourth dimension, the tube is open on its sides just as a drawing of a tube on a sheet of paper, which is two dimensional, is open to our gaze. An object dropped into the bottle will fall out of the tube into the fourth dimension, then enter the next lower space of three dimensions."

"Let me get this straight," said the Scarecrow, "are you telling me that if we can build a Klein Bottle large enough for a person to climb into, he or she will fall down the bottle's tube, drop out of the tube into a four-dimensional space, then fall through that space and land on Earth?"

"Precisely, Scarecrow. Your brains operate more efficiently than I realized. If a large Klein Bottle can be constructed, the next step is to determine where in Oz to place it so that anyone falling through it will land on the earth at whatever spot is desired."

"But who in Oz can build such a fantastic thing?"

"It would be difficult to make out of wood because the bottle consists of curved surfaces, but it should be possible to make it from flexible sheets of tin. I suggest you contact Ku-Klip, the Munchkin tinsmith who made the Tin Woodman's head and body. He can make anything with his high quality tin."

"I'll go see him next week," said the Scarecrow. "You've been a great help, Professor. "May I keep this sketch?"

"Certainly. Please convey my fondest regards to Ozma and Dorothy."

The straw man folded the sheet twice and slid it into a side pocket. He thanked the professor warmly while he shook the bug's long slender fingers.

"If I can be of any further assistance," said H. M. Wogglebug T. E. as the Scarecrow left his office, "don't hesitate to let me know."

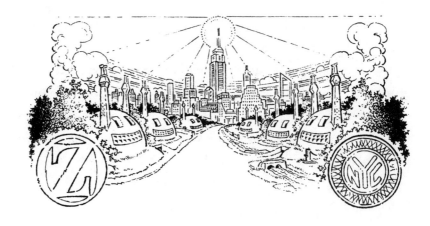

3

KU-KLIP MAKES
THE BOTTLE

WOULD YOU care to join me on my trip to see Ku-Klip?" the Scarecrow asked his tin friend.

"I would indeed," he replied. "It's been a long time since I visited that wonderful tinsmith. You may recall that when I last saw him I had a very confusing conversation with my former head."

"I remember. And didn't you also visit your old sweetheart Nimmie Amee?"

"I did. She seemed happily married to someone named Chopfyt. Ku-Klip had glued him together with parts of my meat body and parts of the meat body of Captain Fyter. Remember Fyter? He had met with the same terrible fate I did. The same evil witch enchanted his sword and each time it cut off part of his body Ku-Klip would replace the part with tin. It was my good luck that Chopfyt got Captain Fyter's original head, not mine. Otherwise, I suppose that in a way I would now be Nimmie Amee's husband as well as being the Tin Woodman of Oz."

"Stop!" exclaimed the Scarecrow. "Please, no more talk about who's who. It befuddles my brains and gives me a headache. Do you know where the Tin Soldier is now?"

"Yes, he's living somewhere in the northeast corner of the Gillikin country. Ozma sent him there many years ago to keep order among the rowdy Gillikins."

The two old friends arranged to make the journey to Ku-Klip's workshop in Ozma's Red Wagon. The wagon was always pulled by the Sawhorse, a famous Oz resident, who came to life in *The Land of Oz* when the boy Tip—he later turned out to be Ozma in enchanted form—sprinkled the Powder of Life on an ordinary wooden sawhorse. Much to the sawhorse's amazement, he suddenly found himself alive.

The Sawhorse stood motionless, waiting for orders, while the Scarecrow and the Tin Woodman climbed into the Red Wagon's front seat. The straw man's face had been freshly painted for the trip, and the tin man's newly polished body glinted in the morning's bright sunshine.

Ku-Klip's home and workshop were at the edge of the Great Blue Forest in the southwest region of Munchkin country. It took the Scarecrow and Tin Woodman several days, riding in the Red Wagon through beautiful blue farmlands, before they reached Ku-Klip's home.

"Would you like to come with us?" the straw man asked the Sawhorse, as he and his friend climbed down from the wagon.

"Thanks, but no," said the Sawhorse. "I'll wait here and think."

"What do you think about?" asked the tin man.

"Oh, mostly about some of the wild adventures I've had since Ozma shook that dreadful Powder of Life over me."

"You couldn't have had those adventures if you hadn't been brought to life."

"I suppose you're right. Maybe it's not so bad after all to be alive and to know you're alive."

The two visitors walked around Ku-Klip's modest tin-frame house to the back where he had built a huge workshop. They found the famous tinsmith seated at a long bench, where he was painting a dozen tin birds blue. They were anxious to be released so they could test how well their metal wings would operate.

Ku-Klip was a large elderly man with a long white beard that reached almost to his feet. The thick lenses of his spectacles greatly magnified his eyes.

"It's good to see you again, Nick," Ku-Klip said as he stood up and wiped his hands on a blue apron. He was, of course, using the original first name of Nick Chopper before his body had been replaced by Tin. "You and Captain Fyter are my finest works of art. How's that silk velvet heart of yours doing?"

"It beats as strongly and regularly as ever," answered Nick. "Do you remember my old friend the Scarecrow?"

"I do indeed," said the tinsmith as he shook the straw man's cloth hand. "You were along when Nick last visited me. As I told you then, any time you please I can replace your straw and cloth with excellent working parts made of tin. You won't have to be afraid of fires. Once your body is nickel plated, even bullets can't dent you."

"It's good of you to suggest it again," said the Scarecrow, "but I prefer the way I am. I may not have a kind heart like my friend here, but I do have brains that work much better than those tin brains you gave him."

Ku-Klip turned to the Tin Woodman. "I make much better brains now than I could years ago. If you like, I can replace your present brains with superior new ones."

"Perhaps some other time," said Nick, as he leaned his axe against the side of Ku-Klip's workbench. "I've observed that persons with top-quality brains waste lots of time worrying about this and that, trying to understand everything about the world and about themselves. I really don't give a tinker's damn about whether there's life on other planets, and I don't waste hours playing ridiculous games like chess and bridge. I'm happy not to understand thousands of things as long as I can love all living creatures and be as kind to them as I can."

Ku-Klip turned to the straw man. "Would you consider letting me give you a tin heart?"

"I would not. A heart would only make me unhappy thinking about all the terrible things that happen to people on Earth and even sometimes in Oz—things I can't do anything about."

"Tell me," said the Tin Woodman, "how's my old sweetheart Nimmie Amee these days? It's been ages since I visited her and her husband, Chopfyt. You may have read about this in the book by L. Frank Baum that he named after me, *The Tin Woodman of Oz.*"

"I haven't read it," said the tinsmith with a shake of his

That is 'Tinker's dam': a small ring of clay placed around a hole in a pot. This dam restrains the molten metal used to repair the hole. — and hence, an item of negligible intrinsic value.

head that made his whiskers wobble, "or any other book about Oz. To tell the truth, I never learned how to read. As for Nimmie, I haven't seen her for years. I'm told she's as pleased as ever with that meat husband I glued together for her, even though Captain Fyter's head tends to be surly most of the time."

"And how about *my* former head?"

"You'll be pleased to know that I felt so sorry for that old head of yours being cooped up so long in a dark cupboard that I made a splendid tin body for it. Your head has taken the name of Nick Tinsley. Last year he married Nimmie Amee's sister Bonny. Now he's back at his old trade. As you must know, our Blue Forest supplies most of the wood for houses and furniture in the Emerald City. Tinsley enjoys his work much more than when he was made of meat. His muscles never get tired. He can chop down trees for as long as he likes without getting sore arms or backaches."

"I'm delighted to hear that," said the tin man. "I always felt terrible about the plight of my old head."

"Enough of this chit-chat," said Ku-Klip, taking off his thick glasses to wipe them on his apron. "Tell me—why did you two come all the way down here to see me?"

"Ah, yes," said the Scarecrow, who had been listening quietly without saying anything. Trying to understand how Nick Chopper could be two different men made him very uncomfortable. He was glad to change the subject. For the next ten minutes he told Ku-Klip about their plans to join Dorothy on a vacation in the United States and how in order to get there they needed a curious object called a Klein Bottle.

"I can't imagine why you'd want to visit America," Ku-Klip said. "Its cities swarm with murders and suicides and muggings and car crashes and airplane disasters. The people in the United States, I'm told, have all sorts of crazy beliefs— astrology, flying saucers, reincarnation, and hundreds of other ridiculous things. Some of them even think they can cure ailments by sticking long needles into their body."

"No one can stick a needle in *my* body," said the tin man. "It would be easy to stick needles into Scarecrow, but I doubt if it would improve his health."

"Now about that Klein Bottle," said Ku-Klip. "Of course I can make one provided I see a good picture of it. I can make anything out of tin."

The Tin Woodman opened a small door he recently had made in his chest so he could carry things inside. He reached into the opening and removed a folded sheet of paper that the Scarecrow had given to him for safekeeping. He unfolded it and handed it to the tinsmith.

"Here's a drawing of a Klein Bottle that Professor Wog- glebug sketched for Scarecrow. I hope you can understand it."

Ku-Klip adjusted his spectacles and studied the drawing silently for several minutes. He turned it upside down, frowned, then turned it sideways. "It's certainly a peculiar structure. However, I'm sure I can construct it. You must allow me at least three weeks. I won't get to it until I replace your cat—excuse me, I mean Mr. Tinsley's cat—with tin. The poor cat was almost eaten last month by one of the drag- ons that still roam our Blue Forest. Tinsley and his wife, Bonny, have begged me to replace their damaged cat with tin. They assume no dragon will try to eat a tin cat. I suppose he's right."

"Be sure to make the bottle large enough so we can slide through its tube," said the Scarecrow.

"Don't worry. I'll make a huge bottle. I have no idea how the thing works, but I'll take Wogglebug's word that it will get you three to the United States. Will you come to pick it up?"

"I'll probably come alone," said the straw man. "Please telephone Ozma just as soon as the bottle is finished."

The tin man picked up his axe, and the two friends left to rejoin the Sawhorse. He had been waiting patiently outside, chatting with a blue butterfly that rested for a while on his nose. The butterfly fluttered away when she saw the two men approach.

It was more than a month before Ku-Klip let Ozma know that the bottle was finished. "I sometimes think that my wood brains are better than yours," the Sawhorse said to the Scarecrow as he climbed into the Red Wagon for a second trip to Ku-Klip's workshop. "You must be out of your senses to get into that bottle and expect to land on Earth."

When the Scarecrow saw the bottle he noticed something very strange. Near the bottle's base, where its tube twisted through the fourth dimension, there was a gap of empty space. The tube ended abruptly about a yard from the bottle's side, then it reappeared inside the bottle.

"Getting that tube to twist out of our space and back into the bottle wasn't easy," said Ku-Klip. "I had to phone Professor Wogglebug for help. He couldn't explain it over the phone so he asked Ozma to use her Magic Belt to send me one of the Wizard's topology pills. As soon as I swallowed it I understood at once how to do it."

The Scarecrow moved his hand back and forth through the tube's mysterious gap. His hand vanished as long as it was inside the gap. He couldn't feel a thing.

"I understand why you're so mystified," said Ku-Klip. "One needs training in topology to know how the bottle works. I myself was completely puzzled until I swallowed that topology pill. Out of curiosity, I tested the bottle by dropping a large rock into it. I could hear it rattle down the tube, then there was a bang like a gun going off. I assume the rock must have dropped out of the tube and fallen somewhere on the earth."

As author of this book, I can tell you exactly what happened. Down on Earth the rock landed on the roof of a tobacco farmer's house near Winston-Salem, North Carolina. The farmer thought it was a meteorite from the skies. His wife suspected some mischievous boy in the neighborhood had thrown it.

The farmer took the rock to the geology department of the University of North Carolina, at Chapel Hill. He was told it could not possibly be a meteorite because it was made of limestone. When the rock was split in half, it was found to contain fossils of worms never before seen. Each worm had three heads!

The geology department sold the specimen to the American Museum of Natural History, in New York. The museum's paleontologist, Stephen Jay Gould, wrote a paper about the discovery. He ended by saying that although the rock surely came from the earth's Cambrian period, the fossil worms were so unusual he could only conclude that the rock must have come "straight from Oz."

The Klein Bottle was much too large to rest on the benches of the Red Wagon without toppling off. Ku-Klip provided some stout rope made with braided strands of tin, then he and the Scarecrow managed to tie the huge bottle firmly to the wagon's rows of seats. This left no place for the straw man to sit, so he was forced to ride on the Sawhorse. On the way back to the Emerald City he fell off several times when the horse galloped around a sharp curve. Being made of straw, of course it never injured him.

"Ku-Klip should have tied *you* to *me*," said the Sawhorse.

Back at the Emerald City, Professor Wogglebug was pleased with how well the Klein Bottle had been made. "We must now determine, he said to the Scarecrow, "exactly where in the United States you plan to land."

"That's already been decided," said the Scarecrow. "Samuel Gold has an apartment in Manhattan, on Fifth Avenue—that's a street which runs, I'm told, north and south along the east side of a large park called Central Park. He wants us to enter the park late at night when not many people will be around to see us drop down from the sky. He plans to meet us there at three in the morning. The day has yet to be selected. Can you tell me where in Oz we must take the bottle so it will be directly over Central Park?"

"I can tell you in a jiffy," said the bug, "as soon as I swallow one of the Wizard's geography pills."

Professor Wogglebug woggled over to a back wall of his office and took a bottle of pink tablets down from a shelf in a wall cupboard. After washing it down with a drink of water, he blinked his big bulging eyes several times before he said: "The place to put the bottle is in the northeast corner of the Gillikin country near the village of Ballville."

"Ballville?" said the Scarecrow. "That's a town I never heard of."

The wogglebug liked to improvise limericks. He thought for a few moments, then recited:

In Ballville a red rubber ball
Like Humpty fell off a high wall.
She bounced for a while,
Then said with a smile,
"I'm not even scratched by the fall."

Back in Ozma's palace, when Dorothy was told about Ballville, she, too, claimed to know nothing about the town. "There are thousands of strange places in Oz that even Ozma doesn't know about," Dorothy said to the straw man. "Did the wogglebug tell you what sort of people live there?"

"Yes, the geography pill informed him that the town is inhabited by balls—every kind of ball used in playing indoor and outdoor games."

"You mean the balls are alive?"

"I assume so."

"How interesting. I love Ozzy towns. It should be great fun to visit Ballville."

4

MOUNT OLYMPUS

IF YOU read the Royal Historian's book *Rinkitink in Oz* you will be familiar with the three enchanted pearls. Because the King of Pingaree had saved a Mermaid Queen from her enemies, she rewarded him with a gift of three powerful magic pearls. The blue-tinted pearl gave superhuman strength to whoever carried it. The pink-tinted pearl protected its bearer from all harm. And the white pearl could speak and give wise advice.

"Do you remember," said Ozma to Dorothy, "how those pearls saved the life of Prince Inga? Well, a few years ago, at one of my birthday parties, Prince Inga and his friend King Rinkitink were here as honored guests. Inga told me that everything was so peaceful on the Island of Pingaree that he no longer needed the pearls. He gave them to me as a birthday present. I keep them locked securely in my safe."

Dorothy watched while Ozma twiddled the knob on a wall safe concealed behind a portrait of Glinda. After turning the knob back and forth to seven numbers, 5-13-5-18-1-12-4, she swung open the steel door and took out a small green silk bag. It contained the enchanted pearls, each the size of a marble.

"I'm lending these to you for your trip to Earth," Ozma said as she handed the bag to Dorothy. "Guard them well."

Following Ozma's instructions, Dorothy put the blue pearl in the tip of her right shoe, and the pink pearl in the tip of her left shoe. She expected them to be uncomfortable, but part of their magic was that her toes could not feel them at all. The white pearl she held to her ear.

"Take good care of me and my sisters," the pearl whispered in a strange accent. "We wish you a happy and safe visit to the wicked city of New York."

Dorothy returned the white pearl to the silk bag. She closed the bag by pulling a long loop of gold cord, then hung the cord around her neck. She pushed the bag inside her blouse where it could not be seen.

"The pearls operate as often as needed when they are inside Oz and its surroundings," Ozma said, "but on Earth each pearl can be used only once. If you use it, it will fly back to my safe as soon as its work is finished."

Dorothy was so grateful for the loan of the pearls that she gave Ozma a hug and a kiss on the cheek.

"I have something else for you to take," said Princess Ozma. She reached into the safe again to remove a silver ring set with a large emerald. "The Wizard made this for me many decades ago. As you see, it's an exact duplicate of the ring I'm wearing."

Ozma held up her left hand to show Dorothy the emerald ring on her middle finger. "If you press the emerald on the ring I just gave you it will turn bright red. When that happens, the emerald on my ring will also turn red and start to chime like an old-fashioned clock. It will be a signal to me that you're in grave danger. I'll rush to my Magic Picture and ask it to show me where you are. As soon as I see what's happening, I'll press the emerald on my ring. This will cause *your* ring to chime. When you hear it chime you'll know that I've put on my Magic Belt."

Ozma paused to point to a jeweled belt hanging on a peg next to the Magic Picture. The picture was blank, like the screen of a television set that has been turned off.

"Once I have on my Magic Belt," Ozma continued, "I'll be able to do whatever is necessary to rescue you."

"I didn't know your Magic Belt still worked on events outside Oz," said Dorothy. "I realize it's powerless now to teleport persons from Oz to Earth, or from Earth to Oz."

"True. However, my belt still has the ability to move persons and objects on Earth from one place to another, as well as to do many other wonderful things."

Dorothy slipped the emerald ring on the third finger of her left hand. "Thanks, again, Ozma. You're a dear friend. I hope I won't need to use either the pearls or the ring."

"I hope so, too. But I'm sure you know even better than I that the outside world is far more dangerous than any part of Oz. You may be glad you have those pearls and the ring."

"Because you won't be able to teleport us back to Oz,"

Dorothy said, "I assume we'll have to return by climbing up through that Klein Bottle. Professor Wogglebug says its tube will be invisible on Earth so it won't be easy to find. Besides, even if we do find it, will we be able to climb up through it? There isn't anything inside to grab on to."

"I'm sure, my dear, you'll be able to manage somehow."

Before starting their trip to Ballville, Dorothy and her two companions unfolded a large map of Oz that Professor Wogglebug had prepared long before Glinda moved Oz off the earth. They studied it carefully.

"Ballville is about a thousand miles from the Emerald City," Dorothy remarked as she pressed a fingertip on Ballville's spot on the map. "It's in the far northeast corner of the Gillikin country, close to where the Munchkin-Gillikin border meets the Deadly Desert. Assuming the Sawhorse runs at his usual speed of eighty miles per hour, we should be able to reach Ballville in two or three days."

"Provided we aren't delayed along the way," added the Scarecrow. "There are many strange villages near the roads we'll be traveling—villages none of us has visited before. We may be tempted to stop and investigate."

"Right you are, my friend," said the Tin Woodman. "The Tin Soldier—he's in charge, you know, of keeping order among the Gillikins—once informed me that his country is the least explored in all of Oz."

"I've asked Glinda," said Dorothy, "to tell Mr. Gold we can't let him know the exact time of our arrival in New York City until we reach Ballville and have the Klein Bottle placed in the ground. I wouldn't want to miss any exciting adventures along the way."

After Dorothy packed her suitcase, the tin man carried it,

along with a sleeping bag, to the Red Wagon. A large yellow cart, for transporting the Klein Bottle, had been hitched to the rear of the Red Wagon. Using the braided tin rope that Ku-Klip had provided, the Scarecrow and the tin man tied the bottle firmly on the Yellow Cart.

The Tin Woodman helped Dorothy climb onto the front bench of the Red Wagon, then he and the straw man took a seat on either side of her. After being told which road to take, the Sawhorse began with a slow trot until he reached the city's outskirts, then he increased his speed to a fast gallop. The Wizard had long ago installed a glass windshield at the front of the wagon. Otherwise a strong wind would have blown the Scarecrow off his seat, and Dorothy would have found the wind unbearable against her face and her soft blond hair.

It was a warm morning of strong sunlight and fragrant breezes. After traveling for several hours through the purple Gillikin hills, the Red Wagon and the Yellow Cart came to an intersection of twisting roads where a large sign pointed to a small mountain not far away. The sign's purple letters said: MOUNT OLYMPUS, HOME OF THE GREEK GODS.

"Who are the Greek gods?" asked the Tin Woodman.

"We learned about them in school," said Dorothy. "They were worshiped for centuries by the ancient Greeks and later by the Romans."

"And who were the Greeks and Romans?" asked the Scarecrow.

Dorothy did her best to tell her friends most of what she could remember about the Greek gods, and how the Romans continued to worship them under different names.

"Surely those gods were not real persons," said the straw man. "And even if they were, what are they doing here in Oz?"

"Let's find out," said Dorothy, always eager for a new adventure.

The Sawhorse was annoyed by the delay in plans, but he always obeyed orders. The travelers were surprised to see that the road led to a huge, beautiful castle, its tall purple towers glittering in the sunlight.

"Try to make your visit short," said the Sawhorse, as Dorothy and her friends hopped off the Red Wagon. "I get bored and irritated if I have to stand still for hours."

The travelers crossed a small bridge that arched over a moat of dark water. As they approached the castle's entrance, a heavy bronze door swung open and a small man emerged. One of his legs was shorter than the other. It made him walk with a limp.

"Welcome to our castle," said the little man with a low bow. "Mercury saw you coming, and our Oracle told us who you are. My name is Vulcan. His majesty Jupiter awaits your presence."

As they followed Vulcan down a long corridor lined with marble statues, Dorothy whispered to her friends: "Vulcan was one of the sons of Jupiter and his wife, Juno. He was born crippled. He's a very talented carpenter and metal worker. He made Jupiter's sceptre and all sorts of other beautiful and wonderful things."

"I doubt if he could have made me," said the Tin Woodman. "Only Ku-Klip could have done that."

In the large throne room they came upon Jupiter, also known as Jove and Zeus, and his handsome wife, Juno. They sat side by side on two thrones. Jupiter was a giant of a man with deep black eyes and a mop of black curls surrounding his head. An eagle was perched on his left shoulder.

"I know how surprised you must be to find us living here," Jupiter said. "After Rome fell, and Christianity became the religion of Europe, people stopped believing in us. As a result we lost almost all our powers. To tell you the truth, we nearly faded away, but because we're immortal we were unable to die. We couldn't bear staying in a place where nobody believed we were real."

Dorothy and her friends listened in wonderment as Jupiter continued. "Almost two thousand years ago, long before Glinda took Oz off the earth, we decided to pack up our belongings and move here. It was the only land where we thought we could live in peace."

"How did you manage to cross the Deadly Desert?" Dorothy asked.

"The same way your Wizard did. Vulcan constructed a giant dirigible, the first one ever made. It floated all of us over the deadly sands. We settled at the foot of this mountain and named it Olympus. Of course it's not nearly as large as the one in Thessaly where we lived for thousands of years."

Juno, who was wearing a crown decorated with peacock feathers, jabbed her husband's side with her elbow. "It was millions of years, you idiot. Try to keep your facts straight."

"Yes, my love, it was millions," Jupiter sighed. His deep bass voice sounded sad. "You're always right, my dear."

"You said you lost *almost* all your powers," said the Scarecrow. "Does that mean you still have some left?"

"It does," said the king. "For example, I was able once to send terrible thunderbolts of lightning down on Earth. They could kill people and destroy entire cities. Now the best I can do is this...."

Jupiter shifted his jeweled sceptre to his left hand, then held out his right hand and extended its fingers. Sparks jumped from the fingertips, making little crackling sounds. The Scarecrow leaped back in terror. Even the smallest spark, he knew, could set him on fire.

"Don't worry, Scarecrow," said the king. "Those sparks are as harmless as sparks from the sparklers American children light on the Fourth of July."

"You'll notice," said the eagle on the king's shoulder, "that my master's sparks don't even frighten *me*. I can remember how terrified I used to be when he hurled his great thunderbolts on the Greeks and Romans. Now they wouldn't harm a hummingbird."

"I used to have wonderful powers, too," said Juno. "Now they're gone. All gone. My good friend Iris, the rainbow goddess, lost all her powers completely. They were taken over by that dancing imposter Polychrome. If I ever get my hands on her, I'll bash her pretty face."

"Now, now, my love," said the king, patting his wife's arm. "Try to control that terrible temper of yours. For all we know our visitors may be good friends of Polychrome."

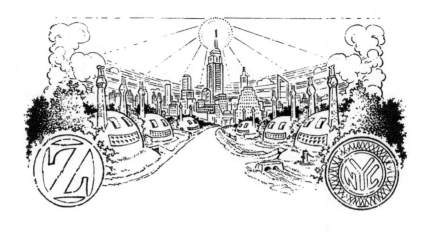

5

A BANQUET WITH THE GODS

A HANDSOME young man, dressed in a white toga like the other gods, entered the throne room. Small wings were attached to each side of his gold sandals—wings that once enabled him to fly like an eagle. Now they were no more than fancy decorations.

"I'm Mercury," he informed Dorothy. "They call me the messenger of the gods. Please follow me. I'll take you to your rooms where you can freshen up and relax before dinner. Then I'll escort you to our dining hall. We have a grand feast prepared for you and your distinguished companions."

"My straw friend and I neither eat nor drink," said the Tin

Woodman, "but we'll enjoy the conversation. Dorothy must be hungry after riding for hours in a bumpy wagon."

"Yes," said Dorothy. "I'm famished."

The banquet guests were seated around an enormous oval table. They all stood up when the visitors entered the hall. Venus rushed over to Dorothy to hug and kiss her.

"I love the smell of your hair," Venus said. "And what a gorgeous emerald ring you're wearing."

"Thank you. It's not really mine. Ozma let me borrow it for our trip."

Venus was young and strikingly beautiful, with shining blue eyes and flowing yellow hair that grazed her bare shoulders. There was no trace of makeup on her face. She turned to embrace first the Scarecrow then the Tin Woodman.

"My, your body is cold," Venus said to the tin man. "But I'm told you have a warm and loving heart."

"It's a kind heart," said the woodman, "but not as loving as I hoped it would be."

"I'm sure that isn't true," said Venus. "All kind hearts are loving hearts."

The Scarecrow held the chair for Dorothy until she was seated. The Tin Woodman carefully placed his axe on the floor before he sat down.

On the King's left was Juno, looking very stern. On his right sat Neptune, god of the sea. Leaning against the table by his side was the long trident he always carried with him, just as the Tin Woodman always carried his axe.

There were many other gods seated around the vast table. Among them was Pluto, who lived in a deep cave outside the castle. At one time his dog Cerberus was a fierce beast with three heads and a snake for a tail. Now he was a meek single-headed bulldog who wagged his tail and thanked his master whenever he was slipped some food from the table. Hades, which Pluto once ruled and Cerberus guarded, long ago had vanished because no one believed anymore that it existed.

The food consisted mainly of varieties of ambrosia. It had a marvelous taste, unlike any food Dorothy had ever tasted. Dionysus filled the glasses of everyone except those of the straw man and the tin man. The liquid was a milky white wine the gods called nectar. Dorothy noticed that Dionysus's nose was red like the nose of persons overly fond of alcoholic beverages.

Apollo sat next to the Scarecrow. In ancient times, he said, he used to take the sun around the earth, but he had to stop doing this when astronomers proved that the earth went around the sun. On his shoulder hung a quiver of sharp-pointed arrows. He couldn't believe that the person next to him was stuffed with straw. Taking an arrow from the quiver, he jabbed its point into the Scarecrow's side.

"Did that hurt?"

"Not a bit," said the straw man. He took the arrow from Apollo, turned it around, and poked the god's shoulder.

"Did *that* hurt?"

"It certainly did," said Apollo with a wince. He took back the arrow and returned it to the quiver. "I didn't mean any harm, Scarecrow. I was just testing to see if you really are cloth stuffed with straw."

"You can poke me with an arrow also," said the Tin Woodman, who was seated by the Scarecrow. "I won't feel it either. My nickel-plated body will even stop bullets. Besides, like my friend here, I don't have any nerves to send pain to my head."

Apollo stood up and tapped the side of his glass with a

spoon to get attention. "I have a sonnet I would like to read. I composed it last night when our Oracle informed us we should expect visitors. My friend Orpheus tells me he will set it to music."

Apollo took a sip of nectar, cleared his throat, then recited the following poem:

> *Forgotten gods! Alas, the words convey*
> *Too well the dreadful reason for our flight.*
> *No angel host has fallen from the height*
> *From whence we fell. Great gods who held the sway*
> *Of kings and empires now are but the play*
> *Of scholars. Altars once so warm and bright*
> *With sacrificial blood beneath the light*
> *Of ancient moons, lie crumbling, cold and gray.*
>
> *Yet far beyond the vast Olympian snows,*
> *In Oz we gods of Greece are living still.*
> *And Jove in drowsy indolence still nods*
> *His shaggy head in silence. Our repose*
> *Is deep and calm, unbroken by the chill*
> *Of disbelief. For who can kill the gods?*

Apollo bowed slightly in response to prolonged applause.

A few seats from Apollo sat Hercules, a huge man with bulging arm muscles. He explained to the guests how he kept in shape by lifting weights, and by jogging three times around Mount Olympus every morning at sunrise. Later in the day he demonstrated his strength by raising Dorothy high in the air with one hand.

Atlas was seated next to Hercules. He spoke about how

pleased he was when astronomers proved that the earth was suspended on nothing, and he no longer was needed to hold it up.

Athena, with her sea gray eyes, was as beautiful as Venus. She strongly deplored the way education in Oz was declining. "Most college graduates in Oz don't even know the moon rises and sets like the sun, or that it gets its light from the sun. Half of them can't tell you whether Ev is west or east of Oz."

"Maybe it's because they don't have to study anymore," said Dorothy. "They just take the Wizard's learning pills."

"You forget," said Athena, "that the effects of those pills last only a few weeks. The students have no access to the pills after they leave college. That leaves them as ignorant as before."

"She's right," said an owl perched on Athena's shoulder. "It's scandalous. Even I'm smarter than most college students these days. Would you like to hear me recite the multiplication table?"

"We can skip that," said Athena.

"I remember," said Dorothy, "how you saved Ulysses from many perils. We read Homer's *Odyssey* when I was in school."

"Yes," said Athena, tears forming in her gray eyes. "I once had the power to help mortals I liked, and I always liked Ulysses. Now it's all I can do to keep myself out of trouble."

Mars, the brother of Apollo, had a perpetual scowl on his face while he was eating. "He's always angry," Venus explained to Dorothy, "because he no longer can start wars on Earth, although he follows all its wars with great interest. He was delighted with how the Irish were killing each other, and he keeps hoping the Arabs and Jews will have another battle, maybe with atomic weapons."

"How does he know about wars on Earth?" Dorothy asked.

"We have our wonderful Oracle," Venus replied. "She keeps up on all the events in Oz and also events on Earth. It's like the way Glinda's Magic Book of Records keeps *her* informed."

"My son Mars was once a fierce warrior," said Jupiter. "Look at him now. He's a puppy dog."

"That goes for you, too, Father," snapped Mars.

The banquet was followed by an hour of entertainment in a stone amphitheater outside the castle. Hercules displayed his skill at juggling cannonballs. Vulcan amazed everyone with a fire-eating act, followed by several magic tricks using apparatus he had invented and made. There was exotic dancing by a scantily clad Diana, who lived in a forest near the castle.

The goat-footed god Pan played merry airs on his panpipes and told a series of bawdy jokes that made fun of some of the gods in the audience. "Jupiter," he said, "likes to take his wife everywhere, but she always finds her way home." This made the King laugh heartily, but the Queen sat stone-faced. "Not funny," she murmured, as she kicked The King's shin. Orpheus closed the show by strumming his lyre and singing some sad songs he had recently written.

Before the day ended Neptune took Dorothy and her friends on a walk up a spiral path that led to the top of Mount Olympus. The mountain had once been an active volcano. At the top, its crater was filled with the purple water of Lavender Lake. Where the water came from, and where it flowed to, nobody knew.

Neptune stretched out his arms toward the lake and waved his trident. The lake had been as smooth as glass. Now tiny ripples raced over its surface.

"You see," Neptune said with a choke in his voice. "Once I was able to cause violent storms on the world's vast oceans. They were storms that could sink the largest ships. Now the best I can do is make these miserable little waves."

Dorothy and her companions were given two bedrooms where they could stay overnight. The Scarecrow rested in a chair, with a towel over his face to keep from his painted eyes the milky moonlight that was streaming through a window. The Tin Woodman was resting in another chair, his eyes closed, when a huge black spider crawled up his leg and tried to bite him.

"Jumpin' Jupiter!" exclaimed the spider. "I can't believe it! You're made of metal!"

The tin man opened his eyes. "That I am." He reached down and carefully picked up the spider between a finger and thumb.

"Please," the spider whimpered, "don't crush me!"

"No need to worry, Spider. I never harm any of God's living creatures, no matter how small." The woodman carried the spider to the open window and tossed him out on the silver-tinted grass.

Next morning, when the travelers departed, they were sorry to leave. Jupiter and Juno walked them to the Red Wagon.

"It's about time you guys showed up," growled the Sawhorse.

"Who asked you?" said Juno. "Horses should be seen and not heard, especially wooden horses. What in the name of Jove is that ridiculous contraption on the cart?"

"It's called a Klein Bottle," said Dorothy. She tried to explain how it was supposed to work and what their plans were for using it to get to New York.

"Sounds insane to me," said Juno. "You must be out of your mind to want to visit New York."

"When you get to New York," said Jupiter, "please tell the reporters that we gods are alive and well."

"Don't be so naive," said Juno. "You know as well as I do that no one in New York will believe it. From what I've heard about New York, they don't believe anything. Anyway, have a good trip, and Jove bless."

After thanking the King and Queen for their hospitality, the travelers climbed into the Red Wagon and waved good-bye. The Sawhorse yawned, stretched his wooden legs, and began a slow trot before he broke into his rapid stride.

"It's heartbreaking how far those Greek gods have fallen," Dorothy remarked.

"I wonder if what they told us is true," said the Tin Wood-man. "They could be clever imposters, like those charlatans who go around the Emerald City pretending to be The Wizard or Glinda. If so, is it possible they actually think they are Greek gods? Maybe they deceive themselves. Maybe they no longer can tell the difference between the real world and fantasy."

"You could be right," said the Scarecrow, "but whether they're frauds or not, I learned a lot about what Dorothy says the Earthlings call the great myths of Greece and Rome."

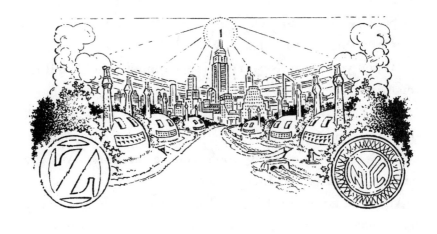

6

WONDERLAND

AFTER TRAVELING several hours of the morning through a violet-tinged mist, Dorothy and her companions noticed a small building ahead. Not until they got closer could they read through the mist a sign on top of the building. It said ENTRANCE TO WONDERLAND.

"Could this be the Wonderland Alice visited in her dreams?" Dorothy wondered aloud. "When I was a child, Auntie Em read two strange books to me about Alice's adventures. I didn't much like them. The scenes kept changing too suddenly, like real dreams I suppose. And the characters Alice met were so unpleasant to her."

"I never heard of those books," said the Tin Woodman. "But not many books by writers outside of Oz get published in Oz. Baum's Oz books are rare exceptions. Why don't we stop and investigate Wonderland?"

"Here we go again," growled the Sawhorse. "We'll never get to Ballville if we keep stopping to visit every ridiculous town along the way."

The Sawhorse halted in front of the little building, then stood silent and motionless while the three travelers got down from the Red Wagon and walked to the building's door. A large brass knocker was shaped like the head of a rabbit. Dorothy rapped it several times.

The door was opened by a white rabbit wearing a checkered jacket over a vest with a gold chain that looped across it from pocket to pocket. He looked startled. "You must be one of Oz's many humans," he said. "Your name?"

"I'm Dorothy Gale. Originally I came from Kansas, but now I'm a permanent citizen of the Emerald City."

"Kansas?" said the rabbit with a frown and a twitch of his long ears. "Is that near Oxford, England, where Lewis Carroll lived?"

"No, it's a state in the United States."

The rabbit nodded. "I've heard of the United States. A dreadful country. How in the world did you manage to get across the Deadly Desert?"

"It's a long story," said Dorothy.

"Well, you don't need to tell me now. But please, Miss Gale, who are these weird-looking creatures with you?"

"They're my dearest friends. This is the Scarecrow and this is the Tin Woodman." The two men extended hands to shake the rabbit's paw.

"Your hand feels like it's stuffed with straw," said the White Rabbit.

"My entire body is stuffed with straw," the Scarecrow replied proudly. "And I have a fine set of brains made with bran. They were given to me by the Wizard."

"I've heard of the Wizard, but I never heard of a scarecrow that came alive."

"Neither did I until it happened. I still don't know how or why it happened. Anyway, it was Dorothy who saw me on the side of the Yellow Brick Road and took me down from the pole that was stuck up my back."

"And you, sir, seem to be made entirely of metal," the rabbit said as he grasped the tin man's hand.

"Yes, I'm made of the highest quality tin. As you can see, it's been nickel plated and polished to keep me from rusting in damp weather such as we're having now. I don't have as good a brain as my straw friend has, but I have a splendid velvet heart. If you put an ear against my chest you can hear it beating."

"Well, I suppose stranger things have happened in Oz. You must tell me more about your histories some other time. For now, let me welcome you to Wonderland."

Inside the little house was an elevator just large enough for all four to squeeze into. The White Rabbit pushed a purple button below which were the letters *dn*. Dorothy noticed that under a second button the same two letters were turned upside down to spell "up."

While the elevator was moving slowly downward, the rabbit said: "Years ago the only way to enter Wonderland was by falling down a rabbit hole. But too many people got injured when they landed, even when they were dreaming, so we had our Carpenter and his assistant the Walrus construct this excellent elevator."

The elevator stopped so suddenly that it made the tin man's limbs clatter. The rabbit slid open the door to reveal a landscape no longer dominated by purple, but blazing with all the natural colors. Overhead was a cloudless blue sky, though how such a sky could exist underground was something Dorothy never did understand.

"Follow me, please," said the rabbit. "I'll be your guide on a quick tour through our village."

The first creature they encountered was a pink caterpillar. He was sitting on a large mushroom, puffing a hookah and looking just like the picture Tenniel drew in Lewis Carroll's first Alice book.

"I remember you," said Dorothy. "You were in the book my aunt read to me. Are we really in the same land Alice visited?"

"Well, yes and no," replied the caterpillar in a sleepy voice. "Alice didn't come here in person, you know. She went to sleep and had two vivid out-of-body dreams in which her mind was here for a few hours. When she told her friend Carroll about her dreams, he took lots of notes, and later wrote two novels based on his notes. He changed lots of things in Alice's dreams, and added lots of things about Wonderland that aren't true."

The caterpillar pointed the mouthpiece of his hookah at Dorothy. "Carroll, you may remember, called me a blue caterpillar. As you can plainly see, I'm not blue. I'm a beautiful pink like that pink ribbon in your yellow hair. You're obviously a girl, a bit older and taller than Alice when she came here. But . . ."

The pink caterpillar turned the end of his hookah toward the straw man. "But *who* are *you?*"

The Scarecrow did his best to explain.

"And *who* are *you?*" the caterpillar asked the tin man.

After the Tin Woodman told his story, the caterpillar waggled his head from side to side. "We've had plenty of weirdos visit Wonderland, in and out of sleep, but you two take the cake."

"I beg your pardon?" said the Scarecrow. "Where is this cake we're supposed to take?"

The pink caterpillar gave a barely audible chuckle. "There isn't any cake. It's just a figure of speech."

"What's a figure of speech?" asked the Tin Woodman.

"Never mind. It's been a great displeasure to meet all of you. Please don't eat any of my mushroom because one side makes you shrink and the other side makes you grow tall."

"Is that really true?" Dorothy asked.

"No. I just tell visitors that because they expect to hear it. Carroll made it up so he could have Alice get back to her normal size after the liquid in the bottle she supposedly drank made her tiny. Good-bye. Don't bother to come again."

"The caterpillar is in one of his usual surly moods," said the White Rabbit. "Don't let it bother you."

The rabbit led his party down a narrow dirt path to a cottage where a huge frog was guarding the front door. "Welcome to the home of the Ugly Duchess," he croaked as he pushed open the door.

The visitors were greeted inside by the ugliest woman they had ever seen. A baby was fast asleep in her arms.

"You look exactly like your picture," said Dorothy. "Do you really beat that little baby every time he sneezes?"

"I most certainly do *not*," replied the Duchess, a trace of anger in her voice. "When Alice visited here in her first dream, I sang my boy a lovely lullaby that begins like this."

In a sweet soprano voice the Duchess sang:

> *Speak gently, it is better far*
> *To rule by love than fear.*
> *Speak gently, let no harsh words mar*
> *The good we might do here.*

"When Lewis Carroll wrote about me," the Duchess continued, "he changed the beautiful words of that song to a cruel parody about speaking roughly. He assumed his readers would think it funny to portray me as a heartless old duchess who beats babies when they sneeze. I love my little boy dearly. I wouldn't dream of hurting him."

The Duchess bent her head so she could kiss the sleeping baby on his forehead.

"You certainly seem very kind," said the Tin Woodman.

"As a matter of fact, said the Duchess, "not only am I not cruel—I'm not even ugly. This is just a mask I put on for readers of Carroll who come here in their dreams."

The Ugly Duchess reached up to her left ear and pulled off a rubber mask to reveal the face of a gorgeous young woman!

"The moral of this is," she said to her amazed visitors, "you must never judge people by how they look. It's what's in their head and heart that matters. Millions of people really have ugly faces. Those faces are like masks. They conceal the beautiful persons they are inside."

"You are surely right," said the Scarecrow. "People think I'm stupid because I have such a funny-looking face."

"And people think I'm coldhearted," said the tin man, "because my face is made of cold metal."

"I'm glad we all agree," said the Duchess as she noticed that both Dorothy and the White Rabbit were nodding. "But you must run along now. I have to change my baby's diaper and prepare lunch before my husband returns."

"I didn't know you were married," said Dorothy. "The book about Wonderland never mentioned a husband."

"Of course not," said the Duchess. "He would have been out of place in Carroll's peculiar fantasy. Did you think I was just baby-sitting? The Duke and I have been happily married for three hundred years."

"This way," the White Rabbit beckoned. "We shouldn't take up any more of the Beautiful Duchess's time. Next I want you to meet our so-called Mad Hatter."

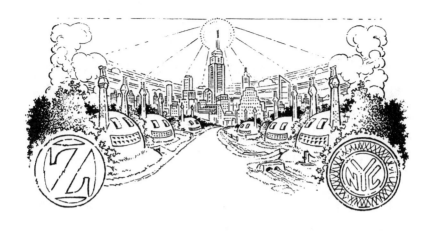

7

THE MAD HATTER

ON THEIR way to the Mad Hatter's house the visitors passed a large pine tree where the Cheshire Cat was sitting on a branch. The cat grinned down at them. "Do you folks know where you're going?"

"We do," said Dorothy. "We're on our way to visit the Mad Hatter."

"Well, you're going in the right direction. If you turned around now and walked the other way you'd get back to where you came from."

"Thank you for such profound advice," said the Scarecrow. "I could have figured that out even if I didn't have a brain."

"I'm sure you could," said the cat. "But it's not the case if you wait too long before you turn around."

"What does that mean?" asked the Tin Woodman.

"It means that everything changes while you wait. Suppose you waited fifty years before you turned around. You would go back to a different place. You can't go home again if enough time goes by. I think a writer in America named Fox wrote a novel about that."

"It wasn't Fox," said the White Rabbit, who had recently swallowed one of the Wizard's American literature pills. "It was Thomas Wolfe. John Fox Jr. was famous for a novel called *The Trail of the Lonesome Pine*."

"Okay, okay," muttered the cat. "I stand corrected."

"You mean you *sit* corrected," said the rabbit.

The cat was about to reply when Dorothy asked, "Can you really disappear and leave only your grin?"

"I can," said the cat. "That's one thing Carroll got right. But at the moment I don't feel like doing it. It's not so easy, you know. It's much easier to vanish and leave only my tail."

So saying, the cat slowly faded away leaving only its tail. As the visitors walked on they heard the cat call out: "It's the tail of the lonesome pine."

The Mad Hatter, seated at a table in his backyard, stood up to greet the visitors. "I've read most of Baum's Oz books, so I know who all of you are. I think our own flawed historian Lewis Carroll would have been fascinated by a live scarecrow and a man made of tin."

"I thought you were a bit crazy," said Dorothy, "but you talk like a perfectly sane man."

"Thank you," said the hatter, with a tip of his top hat. "Of course I'm not mad. That was just another one of the ways Carroll changed Alice's first dream. He wanted to make the dream funnier so he turned me into a moron. I do have as friends a dormouse and a March hare, but they're not mad either. When we have a tea party, by the way, it's only once a day at four o'clock. And our conversation at teatime is as sensible as anybody's in England."

The hatter took a large watch from his vest pocket and held it up. "See, it tells the time of day just like any ordinary watch. Carroll turned it into a watch that showed only the day of the month. It was another way to make me look foolish."

"Did you invent the riddle about the raven and the writing desk?" Dorothy asked.

"I did. After Carroll's book about Wonderland was published, readers thought of lots of clever answers. You can read about them in two books, *The Annotated Alice* and *More Annotated Alice* by the same man who's writing this Oz book. I love to make up riddles. Here's one of my best. What do you sit on, sleep on, and brush your teeth with?"

No one could think of a good answer.

"The answer," said the hatter with a broad smile, "is a chair, a bed, and a toothbrush."

The visitors groaned. "Not fair," said Dorothy. "We thought it had to be one thing."

"Of course you did. That's why you couldn't solve it. Here's a new riddle I invented this morning. What's the difference between a robin and a helicopter?"

After thinking for a while, everyone gave up.

"What's the answer?" the Scarecrow asked.

"I haven't the foggiest idea. If you ever think of a good one, let me know."

The hatter glanced at his watch. "Good gracious! It's time for lunch. Would you care to join me?"

"The straw man and the tin man say they don't eat or drink," the rabbit answered, "but Dorothy and I could use some food."

The hatter led them inside his cottage where his cook, a large ostrich, served a tasty lunch of mock turtle soup, tuna-fish sandwiches, and cherry ice cream.

The White Rabbit's next stop was the palace of the King and Queen of Hearts. Along the road they passed the Jack of Hearts walking the opposite way. Dorothy noticed that his nose was almost as red as the nose of Dionysus.

Jack looked just like his pictures in Carroll's book. He was a large playing card with a face turned so you could see only its left profile. Many of his friends called him "One-eyed Jack."

"I remember," said Dorothy, "that the Queen once ordered your head cut off because you stole some tarts. I'm glad to see you haven't lost your head."

"I never stole no tarts," said Jack. "Carroll made that up so he could work another nursery rhyme into his story. It would, of course, be easy to cut off *my* head. A pair of sharp scissors would do the job."

"Ku-Klip could glue it back on," said the Tin Woodman, "so well that no one could see where your neck had been sliced."

"I'm sure he could. We know all about Ku-Klip, as Humpty Dumpty will probably tell you. Carroll was correct in report-ing that the Queen is always yelling for someone's head to be chopped off, but she never means it. No one in Wonderland has ever been decapitated."

"I'm glad to hear that," said the tin man. "It's a very cruel form of punishment. I would never think of even pulling a wing off a fly. The poor insect would be unable to fly, and would probably be eaten by a bird."

"My friend refuses to go fishing," added the straw man. "Not only because it harms the fish, you understand, but also because he thinks it hurts the worm when you put it on a hook."

The Jack of Hearts stroked the end of his mustache. "I went fishing once. A big fish pulled me into the river. My cardboard got so soaked that I had to lie in the sun for hours until I dried out enough to stand up."

The handsome card shook hands with everyone, then continued on his way. A breeze was blowing so hard that he had to lean to one side at a sharp angle to keep from being blown over.

The White Rabbit led his party across the castle's croquet ground. Dorothy looked around for some sign of flamingos, but there were none to be seen. Carroll had described Alice as trying to use one of the birds as a croquet mallet.

When Dorothy mentioned this to the rabbit, he shook his head. "That's another of Carroll's whimsies. How could anyone possibly hit a croquet ball with the head of a flamingo?"

The Tin Woodman winced at the thought.

A tall Ten of Clubs greeted the visitors at the castle's door and ushered them into the throne room. The King and Queen of Hearts, seated on their thrones, were astonished to see a man made of cloth and straw, and another made of tin. They listened with wonder while each told the story of how he came to be what he was.

"It could only happen in Oz," said the King.

"Off with their heads!" shouted the Queen.

"Calm down, my dear," said the King. He turned to Dorothy. "She likes to say that, but she doesn't mean it. We never execute anyone by any method. Carroll was very unkind to us in his book, especially when he had Alice say we're nothing but a pack of cards."

"But you *are* a pack of cards, aren't you?" said Dorothy.

"Of course we are. It's the 'nothing but' we didn't like. It's true we love to *shuffle* about the palace. Now and then we *cut* ourselves, but life in the palace isn't such a bad *deal*. My wife occasionally dozes off on the throne, but when she does I *poker*. Sometimes I wake her up by pinching the *bridge* of her nose. If you don't believe it you *canasta*. Did you catch all my clever puns?"

"I think I got most of them," said the Scarecrow.

"I'm very good at puns," the King continued while his wife closed her eyes and started to snore. "Try me out. Give me any word."

"How about *umbrella*," said the straw man.

"*Umbrella* glad to meet you."

"*Toothache*," said the tin man.

"I'm thirsty. I need *toothache* a drink."

"*Meretricious*," said Dorothy. She once had heard Professor Wogglebug use that word, though she had no idea what it meant.

"*Meretricious* to you, too," said the King, "and a happy new year."

The White Rabbit, who had left the throne room to chat with some spades in the hallway, returned to tell the guests they had already overstayed their welcome. The King woke his wife with a jab to her ribs. As the visitors left the throne room they heard the Queen screaming "Off with their heads!"

"I don't care much for puns," said Dorothy when they were outside the palace, "though I must admit the King is good at making them."

"He's quite a card," added the Scarecrow.

The White Rabbit led them down a hill and across a stream to where a sign by the road said: THIS WAY TO THE LAND BEHIND THE LOOKING-GLASS.

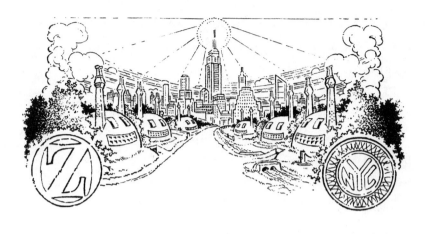

8

HUMPTY DUMPTY

THE ROAD to Looking-Glass Land led to a large two-story house. The White Rabbit took a curious-looking key from a side pocket of his jacket and unlocked the front door. He led the visitors down a long hallway and into an empty living room with an enormous mirror above a stone mantel. A small stepladder stood in front of the fireplace.

"I'll leave you now," said the rabbit. "I hope you enjoyed the tour. Of course you saw only a small part of Wonderland."

"We enjoyed it immensely," said Dorothy. "Thank you for your time and courtesy. But tell us how we get to the other side of this mirror? Do we push through it the way Alice did?"

"That's exactly right. The land behind the mirror is another region of Wonderland. Just climb the ladder, get onto the mantel on your knees, push hard against the glass, and you'll go right through. A ladder will be on the other side to help you down."

Dorothy went first. The Scarecrow and the Tin Woodman watched in amazement as they saw the glass seem to melt while Dorothy passed through it and climbed down the duplicate ladder on the other side. She stood up and waved.

"It's easy," they barely heard her say through the glass. "You won't feel a thing."

Dorothy's pink hair ribbon had been tied on the left side of her head. Now it was on the opposite side.

The two men went next, and were soon standing by Dorothy's side. The room they were in looked exactly like the room they had left except that everything was reversed left and right. The numbers of the clock on the mantel went counterclockwise around its face. The Scarecrow opened a large, leather-bound Bible on a table near the fireplace. It was impossible to read because all its lines were reversed. He held a page up to the mirror. In the reflection the page could be read easily.

The three waved good-bye through the mirror to the White Rabbit, who had been watching. He waved back, checked his watch, then hurried out of the room.

When the visitors walked down the hall and out of the house, they saw before them a vast farmland with crops divided into huge black and white squares like a gigantic chessboard.

The first persons they encountered as they walked along a path were the Tweedle brothers. After the usual introductions and handshakes, Dorothy asked: "Do you two still quarrel over things like a rattle?"

"Of course we don't," snapped Tweedledum. "We never did. Carroll just made that up so he could introduce another nursery rhyme. Like most identical twins, we love each other too much to quarrel about anything."

"You really are identical," said Dorothy. "I certainly can't tell you apart."

"You could if you saw the tops of our heads," said Tweedledee."

The twins took off their caps and bowed low. "Notice," one of them said, "how our hair whirls."

Sure enough, the hair whirled clockwise on one twin and the other way on his brother.

"And your hearts?" asked the Tin Woodman.

"Yes, they too are mirror images," said Tweedledum. "Mine is on the left. My brother's is on the right."

"Mine is on the left," said the tin man, "where it should be."

"Wrong!" shouted Tweedledee. "Don't forget, you went through a mirror. Now it's on the *other* side."

The Tin Woodman opened the little door on his chest and peeked inside. "By golly, you're right! However, it seems to be working as well as it always did."

"Of course," said Tweedledum. "When something is mirror reversed, it's exactly the same as before."

"Only somehow different," said Tweedledee. "It's a funny thing but our magic mirror reverses bodies only, not brains. That's why you can tell your heart has moved to the other side."

"Have you heard the verse about a divinity student named

Tweedle?" asked the Scarecrow. "I read it somewhere years ago in a collection of funny poems. I think I can remember how it goes. Would you like to hear it?"

The brothers nodded.

This is what the straw man recited:

> *A divinity student named Tweedle,*
>   *Refused to accept his degree.*
> *"It's bad enough to be Tweedle," he said,*
>   *"Without being Tweedle D. D."*

Dorothy and the Tin Woodman laughed, but the twins did not even smile.

The White Rabbit was no longer there to guide them, but the visitors assumed they should continue along the path. As they left, the twins waved good-bye, one with his right hand, the other with his left.

"Toodledoo," shouted Tweedledum.

"Teedledee," shouted his brother.

The visitors soon came to a high stone wall on which a huge egg was sitting.

"Why, it's Humpty Dumpty!" exclaimed Dorothy. "I thought you fell off that wall and not even all the king's horses and all the king's men could put you back together."

"Carroll was right about that," said the egg, looking down at the visitors. "But he didn't know what took place *after* my fall. I happen, you know, to be hardboiled. My body wasn't hurt, but the fall broke my shell into six pieces. Glinda read about it in her Magic Book of Records. She and I are old friends. Glinda used to come here to take lessons from me in logic and philosophy. Would you like me to explain how fuzzy logic works?"

"No," said the straw man. "Just tell us what Glinda did."

"Well, Glinda sent two of her flying monkeys to pick me up, along with my shell fragments, and carry me to Ku-Klip. He mended me so carefully with his magic glue that you can't even see the cracks where I broke. I must say, that old tinsmith is a genius."

"He is indeed," agreed the tin man. "But wouldn't it be a good idea to have a net set up at the base of this wall?"

"Oh, that's not necessary. Since my accident I'm *very* careful not to lean forward like I did when Alice was here."

"I liked the way you explained all those nonsense words in 'Jabberwocky,' " said Dorothy.

"Carroll got that all wrong. Alice couldn't recall what I said, so Carroll invented all those silly meanings."

"Can you tell us now what the lines in 'Jabberwocky' really mean?" asked Dorothy.

"No, because they don't mean anything. If they did, the poem wouldn't be nonsense. Carroll wrote it when he was young. How it got to Wonderland I can't imagine. I could make up meanings for the words. As I told Alice, a word can mean anything you want it to mean. But my meanings wouldn't be any better than the ones Carroll put in my mouth. Hundreds of parodies of 'Jabberwocky' have been written, with other strange words, but most of them are not very funny. Would you like me to recite one?"

The visitors nodded.

"I don't know how this one got here either," said the egg. "I'm told it was written by someone named Sam Hair. He lives in Charlotte, North Carolina, wherever that is."

Humpty cleared his throat, adjusted his necktie, and recited the following "Merry Christmas Wocky":

'Twas noel, and the santaclaus
    Did crèche and tinsel in the snow;
All wreathy were the aunts-in-laws,
    And the merry mistletoe.

"I wanta lectrictrain, my dad!
    With car that slides, with track that rocks!
Beware the bricabrac, and shun
    The magi jackinbox!"

He took his blitzen sword in hand:
    Long time the festive foe he sought,
So rested he by the reindeer tree,
    And stood awhile in thought.

And as in holly thought he stopped,
    The lectrictrain, with eyes of flame,
Came yuling through the fruitcaked shop,
    And eggnogged as it came.

One, two! One, two! And through and through
    The blitzen blade went snicker-snack!
He grabbed it, and, with it in hand,
    He went decembring back.

"And hast thou come with lectrictrain?
    Come to my arms, my gifty dad!
O Christmas day! Yip yip! Hey hey!"
    He caroled in his glad.

'Twas noel, and the santaclaus
  Did crèche and tinsel in the snow;
All wreathy were the aunts-in-laws,
  And the merry mistletoe.

When Humpty spoke the last line he waved his short arms like a windmill, then made a bow. The visitors gasped. The egg had leaned so far forward that he toppled off the wall!

The Scarecrow acted quickly. In a flash he flung himself flat on his stomach at the foot of the wall. Humpty landed softly and safely on the straw man's back.

The egg struggled unsteadily to his feet, so embarrassed that his white shell flushed a deep pink. "How careless of me!" he said in a trembling voice as he ran his hands over his sides to see if there were any cracks. "There's no excuse for my falling again. Thank you, Scarecrow. You saved me another long trip to see Ku-Klip. I really must have the Carpenter and the Walrus fix me a net as the tin man suggested."

"Shall I put you back on the wall?" asked the Tin Woodman.

"Thank you, yes," said the egg, still shaking, "but be careful not to drop me."

"I'll be careful." The tin man leaned his axe against the wall, then picked up Humpty and placed him back where he had been sitting.

Humpty took a few deep breaths, then extended an index finger to shake hands with the visitors as they said good-bye.

"What an eggstraordinary thing to witness," said the Tin Woodman as the three continued down the road.

"You must have been influenced by the King of Hearts," said Dorothy. "That was almost an eggcellent pun."

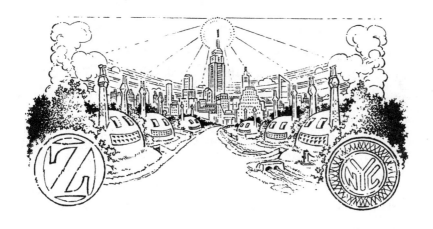

9

THE WHITE KNIGHT

AS THE travelers continued along the path, who should come riding toward them, on a snow white horse, but the White Knight. All sorts of queer looking devices were hanging from both sides of his saddle.

The horse was so startled by the sight of a live scarecrow and a man made of metal that he stopped abruptly. It caused the White Knight to lurch forward and fall to the ground.

"What have we here!" exclaimed the horse. "Are these creatures for real or am I seeing things?"

"They're real enough," said the knight, as he picked himself up, dusted off his armor, and climbed back in the saddle.

"I recognize them from pictures in the Oz books. The girl is Dorothy Gale from Kansas. The two men are the friends she rescued on her way to see the Wizard. That was a long time ago, before the Wizard learned real magic from Glinda, and before Dorothy became a permanent resident of Oz."

"If you ask me," said the horse, "her friends have no right to be alive."

"Nobody asked you," said the Scarecrow.

"What brings you three to Wonderland?" the knight said to Dorothy.

"We're on our way to Ballville. When we saw the sign directing us here we decided to drop down to Wonderland to see what it's like." Dorothy went on to explain about Samuel Gold's invitation to visit America, and how they planned to use the Klein Bottle to get there.

"I never heard of a Klein Bottle," said the knight, "and I don't know much about American cities. When Alice was here she told me a few things about England. It must be a dull place to live."

"It's not dull," said Dorothy. "And the United States isn't dull either. Of course there isn't much magic around, except the fake magic magicians do on the stage, and animals can't talk. Sometimes I wish there wasn't so *much* magic in Oz. There's a lot to be said for places where everything behaves in ways you can expect. It's been a long time since I was in America. I hope I'll get a chance to visit the old farm where I grew up."

"When you say a long time," said the knight, "I assume that when you settled in Oz you decided not to grow any older?"

"Well, not exactly. I let myself reach seventeen. Maybe

sometime I may allow myself to get old enough to marry and have children. But for now I'm staying seventeen."

"That's a fine age for a girl as adorable as you. As for me, I'm not nearly as old as the pictures in Carroll's book make me look. I don't know why Tenniel gave me that walrus mustache. I've never had a mustache. As you can see," he added, lowering his head, "I'm not bald either."

"You really are quite handsome," said Dorothy. "I can understand why Alice was so fond of you. Did you fall in love with her?"

"In a way, perhaps. But you must remember that it wasn't Alice herself who visited us. It was only a dream Alice. It's hard to fall in love with a phantom. But I *did* like her very much. I was sorry to see her leave and wake up back in Oxford."

The knight looked Dorothy up and down. "You, of course, are not a phantom. You're a live flesh-and-blood girl and, I must say, most attractive. I could easily fall in love with *you*. Come back and see me, if and when you decide to grow older. Would you like to take a ride on the back of my horse?"

Dorothy smiled and shook her head. "Thanks, but no. I don't want to leave my friends. Besides, we would like to get back to our wagon while it's still daylight."

"Before you go," said the White Knight, "let me show you my latest invention." He reached into a large bag hanging alongside the saddle and drew out a piece of black pipe about a yard long.

"What is it?" asked the Tin Woodman. He and his friend had been silent while Dorothy and the knight were conversing.

"It's a mousetrap."

The woodman raised his tin eyebrows. "A mousetrap? How does it work?"

"Beautifully. You put a piece of cheese in the middle of the pipe. Then you put the pipe on the floor in a room where mice like to go, and you hide in the next room where you can watch through a crack in the door. As soon as you see a mouse crawl into the pipe, you tiptoe into the room and put a hand over each end of the pipe. Now you've got the little beast trapped. Don't you think it's a very ingenious invention?"

The visitors were too polite to comment.

"How do you dispose of the mouse?" asked the Scarecrow. "Do you drown him?"

The Tin Woodman shuddered at the thought.

"Heavens no! I take him to the woods over yonder." The knight pointed his sword toward a wooded area a few miles away. "Then I let him loose."

"I'm glad to hear that," said the tin man. "It would be unkind to drown a poor helpless mouse. I'm not even sure a mouse can drown in Oz."

"They can't up there," said the knight, pointing upward with his sword. "Down here they can, although it doesn't happen often. I have lots of other clever inventions. They come to me out of the blue while I'm eating or shaving. Last month I invented round dice. If you like, you can use them as marbles. And there's my wonderful whistling toothbrush. When you blow on the end of the handle the toothbrush whistles. You can even put holes along the sides and play it like a piccolo. A few nights ago, when I couldn't sleep, I invented a new kind of compass. Instead of just pointing north it points in *any* direction. And I have hanging here somewhere a pair of shoes I made for walking around inside a house. They make rugs unnecessary."

"My goodness," said Dorothy. "How do they do that?"

"Very simply, my dear. Each shoe has a piece of rug glued to its sole. So, wherever you walk you're always walking on a rug. Don't you think that's a brilliant idea?"

"It certainly is unusual," said Dorothy with a sidelong glance at her friends. She was always reluctant to tell a lie, even if it was a little white one.

"Here's another of my wonderful inventions," said the knight. "It's a silent whistle." He held up an object that looked like a large wooden whistle.

"Why would anyone want a whistle that didn't make a sound?" the Scarecrow asked.

"It could come in handy lots of times. Suppose you're walking down a dark street in the Emerald City, and no thief stops you and tries to steal something. You wouldn't need anyone to come help you, would you? So you just blow on this silent whistle and nobody comes."

Dorothy paused for a moment before she said: "I don't think this is the best time to show us any more of your inventions. It's starting to get dark, and we have to be moving along."

"In that case," said the knight, "would you like to hear me sing a song?"

"No. I remember that dreadful song you sang in Carroll's book. I couldn't understand a single line."

"I can sympathize with you. You should know that I never sang that song. Carroll wrote it himself, though what he had in mind beats me. If you're willing to stay a while longer, I'll sing a romantic song I'm sure you'll understand."

"All right," said Dorothy. "Go ahead, I hope it's not too long."

"Thank you. It's a short song. The lyrics were written by Vincent Starrett, a Chicago poet."

"Is he still living?"

"No, he died years ago. I like to sing his poem to the tune of 'When Irish Eyes Are Smiling.'"

The knight reached into his saddlebag and took out a cassette player. "I'm not good at singing a cappella. This is a recording made by the Munchkin Misfits before they gave up popular music for punk rock."

"I've heard them play," said the Tin Woodman. "Their music is well named."

"I agree," said the knight as he pressed the cassette's start button. When the music for "Irish Eyes" began, he rested the machine on his lap and began to sing in a rich baritone:

> *When you are tired of virtue*
> *And I am tired of sin,*
> *And nothing's left to hurt you,*
> *And nothing's left to win,*
> *Perhaps, O greatly daring,*
> *Your eyes will question mine—*
> *But shall I then be caring*
> *For roses or for wine?*

"I'm glad we stayed," said Dorothy. "That was a splendid song, and you have an excellent voice."

"What was the song about?" asked the Scarecrow. "I didn't quite understand it."

"That's because you don't have a heart," said the tin man.

"I understood it perfectly. It made me think of Nimmie Amee and the days when I had a meat body."

"How do we get back to the upper world?" Dorothy asked. "Do we have to go back through Wonderland the way we came?"

"No," said the knight. He pointed his sword toward a square-shaped building about half a mile down the road. Above it was a tower so tall that it rose upward until it vanished in the cloudless sky.

"There's an elevator inside," the knight continued. "Just press the 'up' button. It will take you back to where you entered Wonderland."

Dorothy waved her handkerchief at the knight as he rode off. When he turned to wave back, he lost his balance and toppled off the horse again.

"I wish you would learn how to ride," said the horse. "You're a disgrace to knighthood. One of these days you're going to fall off me and break some bones. I don't have arms, you know. I can't pick you up and carry you to a hospital."

A red knight on a red horse happened to ride by. The travelers watched him dismount and help the White Knight get to his feet and back on his saddle.

"He was a nice man," said Dorothy. "Maybe a bit goofy, but I can understand why Alice liked him."

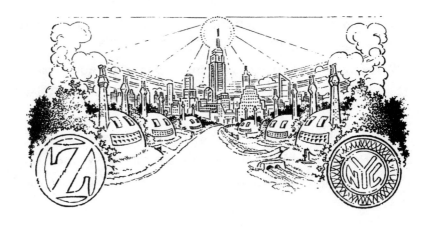

10

—•◦•—

THE RED KING

ON THEIR way to the exit building the three companions came upon the Red King. He was sitting on a large square of black grass, leaning against a tree, sound asleep.

"In Lewis Carroll's *Through the Looking-Glass*," Dorothy said, "the Red King dreams about Alice. And Alice, of course, is dreaming about the Red King. At the end of the story, after Alice wakes up, she wonders whether the King was just a thing in her dream or whether *she's* just a thing in *his* dream. I remember being puzzled and disturbed by this when Aunt Em read the book to me."

"I don't blame you for being disturbed," said the Scarecrow. "I'd hate to think I was just a thing in somebody's dream.

Why don't we wake the king and find out what he's dreaming about now?"

"Good idea," said the Tin Woodman. He walked over to the King and prodded his side with the handle of his axe.

The Red King slowly opened his eyes. He squinted up at Dorothy, rubbed his eyes, then turned his head to look at her companions. "Holy Fisher! You must be Dorothy Gale from Kansas. I recognize you from your pictures in the Oz books."

"Yes, Your Majesty. I'm Dorothy. And these are my old friends the Scarecrow and the Tin Woodman."

The King stood up to shake hands. "It's a great honor to meet all of you. Have I been checkmated?"

"I don't think so," said Dorothy. "You've been asleep and alone. Were you dreaming?"

"Dreaming? Oh my, yes! I've just had a terrible nightmare."

"We'd like to hear about your dream," said the tin man.

The king closed his eyes for a moment. "I'll do my best to remember. I dreamed it was the year 2000. Judit Polgar, the young Hungarian chess grandmaster, had become the world's chess champion. For a payment of three million dollars she accepted a challenge to play against Deep Pink, the world's finest chess computer. The match was held in Budapest. Judit drew the first six of ten games, then lost the next four. She was so furious that she swept all the chess pieces off the table. I dreamed I was the defeated king. It was terrible."

"Why so terrible?" asked the Scarecrow. "You're made of solid ivory. I can't believe you would have been injured by the fall, especially in a dream."

"You don't understand," said the King. "It wasn't my fall

to the floor that was so awful. It was the fall of the Royal Game. Don't you see? After Polgar was so badly defeated by a mindless computer, the public began to lose interest in the game. But that wasn't the end of my nightmare. It got worse."

"Go on," said the tin man.

"Well, Judit was so rattled by losing to Deep Pink that when the next world championship tournament between human players was held in London, she was defeated by Robert Morph, a six-year-old chess prodigy from Brooklyn. That was in 2001. Then a match was arranged between Deep Pink and Morph. By then Pink, using chips made with copper, had become much faster than its predecessor Deep Blue, which used only silicon chips. It could examine in a second billions of possible moves for fifty moves ahead. And it had invented hundreds of wonderful new cooks."

"Cooks?" said Dorothy. "What are cooks?"

"A cook is a surprising new variation of a standard chess opening. It catches opponents off guard. For example, in the Muzio gambit—"

Dorothy interrupted. "None of us here plays chess. We wouldn't know what you'd be telling us."

"I understand. Well, to make a long nightmare short, Deep Pink offered to play Morph without its queen. It won every game!"

The King shuddered at the thought before he continued. "Of course humans continued to play each other for a while, but then it became easy for players to cheat by secretly communicating with computers. When Morph played Stavlokratz, for example, he was soundly beaten. But Stavlokratz played such a flawless game that he was suspected of cheating. The International Chess Federation hired a detective. He discov-

ered that during the match Stavlokratz was sending each of Morph's moves to an accomplice in a nearby hotel."

"How did he do that?" asked the Scarecrow.

"He had a reed switch in the tip of his right shoe. He could press it with his toes. The accomplice was in touch with Deep Pink. Whenever Pink decided on a move, the accomplice would send it to Stavlokratz by pulses he could feel with his left toe. In other words, Morph wasn't playing Stavlokratz. He was playing Deep Pink. No wonder he lost every game."

The King paused to wipe an ivory tear from one eye. "The accomplice was arrested. After he confessed to the swindle, poor Stavlokratz locked himself in a hotel room and put a bullet through his brain. I can still imagine him standing there and pulling the trigger."

"Did the sound of his gun wake you up?" asked the Scarecrow.

"No. I wish it had. But I kept right on dreaming. I dreamed I was talking to Hans Moravic, a man who runs a robot research laboratory somewhere in the United States. He assured me it would be only a few more years until computers would know they were alive. They would be writing great poetry, composing wonderful symphonies, discovering new scientific laws, even writing funny jokes."

"That's not so far-fetched," said Dorothy. "My mechanical friend Tik-Tok can think, speak, and act, just like any meat person."

"I've read about Tik-Tok in Baum's Oz books," replied the King. "As I recall, you found him in a cave in the land of Ev. But Tik-Tok isn't alive. He's a mechanical machine, no smarter than anyone else even when his clockwork is wound, and he's hopeless when it runs down. But according to Moravic, the coming computer robots will be superior to meat people in every way. He thinks the human race will become obsolete and disappear like the dinosaurs. In another century or two only computers will be living on Earth. They will be our mind children. Their destiny will be to explore the universe and colonize other planets."

"I have an excellent brain," said the Scarecrow, "even though it's made of bran and not meat. But I could understand only a small part of your dream. I'm amazed, though, by how much you know about chess-playing on Earth."

"Glinda sends me chess news every week," said the king. "She's on the Internet, you know."

"I wish we could stay longer," said Dorothy, "but it's getting late and we have to be on our way. I hope your nightmare doesn't come true."

"I hope so, too," said the King. "Good-bye. Thanks so much for listening to me so patiently. My wife tells me I talk too much."

Dorothy and her friends hurried toward the exit building. When they looked back, the Red King was sitting, leaning against the tree fast asleep, and snoring loudly.

The elevator in the building looked exactly like the one they rode down in. Dorothy pushed the "up" button. It took almost five minutes for the elevator to reach the top of the shaft. The Tin Woodman opened the door. To their astonishment they walked out of the same little building they had entered earlier!

"How can this be?" the Scarecrow wondered.

"The elevator must have gone sideways as well as up," said the tin man.

Although they had not, as far as they knew, moved through

any kind of mirror, the pink ribbon was now back on the left side of Dorothy's golden hair. The Tin Woodman put his hand on his chest. He could feel his heart thumping on the left side.

The Sawhorse was patiently waiting, hitched to the Red Wagon, which had hooked to it the Yellow Cart that held the Klein Bottle. The sun was low in the west, tinging the clouds violet and casting long dark shadows on the purple grass.

"You've been gone almost nine hours," complained the Sawhorse as he turned his head to watch Dorothy and her friends climb into the Red Wagon. "Let's not stop anywhere again. And please—don't tell me what Wonderland is like. I'm not interested."

"They have real horses there," said Dorothy.

"There you go! Telling me things I don't want to hear even though I asked you not to. I'm sure those horses can't run as fast as I can. I'm sure they're not as smart or as well read as I am. If we expect to reach Ballville by morning we'll have to travel all night. *I* don't mind because I never get tired. But *you'll* have to sleep on a hard bench and your friends will have to stay wide awake and be bored to death. I'll run as fast as I can."

The Sawhorse began a slow gallop while he hummed a popular Oz tune called "The Yellow Brick Ramble." The wind began to blow with tremendous force against the Red Wagon's windshield when the Sawhorse increased his speed to a hundred miles an hour.

11

⟨⟨⟨≈

BALLVILLE

THE BEST spot to place the Klein Bottle so it would be directly over Central Park, Professor Wogglebug determined, was in a clearing about two miles north of Ballville. The clearing was next to the main road and near a gold-tinted stream that flowed over a small waterfall.

It was late in the morning when the Sawhorse reached the waterfall. He halted and glanced back for instructions.

Dorothy was eager to visit Ballville. "There's no need to take the Yellow Cart with us," she said to the Sawhorse. "We'll unhitch it and leave it here until we get back."

"Aren't you afraid someone might steal the bottle?" asked the Scarecrow.

"I can't imagine anyone doing that. What possible use would it be even if the thief knew how it worked? Besides, it's too heavy for one person to carry."

The Tin Woodman unhitched the Yellow Cart. The travelers climbed back into the Red Wagon and Dorothy asked the Sawhorse to take them to Ballville.

Princess Ozma had been monitoring the progress of the travelers by checking them every hour in her Magic Picture. When she saw them approaching Ballville she telephoned Mr. Ballard, the town's mayor, to tell him to expect three distinguished visitors. She explained who they were.

It was approaching noon when the Sawhorse pulled up in front of Ballville's city hall. A small crowd of Ballvillians gathered around the Red Wagon to view with amazement a living man of straw, another made of tin, and a wooden horse. The Mayor himself waddled out of the building to greet his guests.

"No wonder the town's called Ballville!" exclaimed Dorothy. "The people here really *are* balls!"

It was true. The Mayor was a brown bowling ball about ten times the size of an ordinary bowling ball. Small arms and legs projected from his body. Bright green eyes could be seen deep inside the two finger holes. The thumb hole was his nose. He also had a wide mouth and two tiny ears.

"Welcome to our humble town," said Mayor Ballard with a low bow. "We are indeed honored to receive such famous visitors."

The crowd of balls grew larger. Every kind of ball used in both indoor and outdoor games was represented. There were tennis balls, baseballs, softballs, footballs, soccer balls, basketballs, pool balls, rubber balls, croquet balls, volleyballs, golf balls, handballs, polo balls, table-tennis balls, beach balls, and hundreds of enlarged glass marbles.

Never before had Dorothy realized how many games required balls. Maybe they are as necessary for human play, she later speculated, as spheres are necessary to the universe. Could it be that the suns, planets, and moons are required for some kind of vast, inscrutable game?

Dorothy had not eaten since the day before, so she eagerly accepted the mayor's invitation to lunch. After she had freshened up in Mr. Ballard's private bathroom, the mayor led the visitors to a large ballroom he had temporarily converted to a dining hall. A representative of every type of ball in Ballville had been invited. Dozens of circular tables filled the room. Dorothy and her friends were seated at the mayor's table.

Dorothy explained to Mr. Ballard as best she could about the purpose of their trip. She described the Klein Bottle they had brought along, and told how they planned to use it for entering New York City to help a movie producer publicize a new film about Oz.

The Mayor shook his head in wonderment. "It sounds fantastic and dangerous. I certainly hope the bottle works the way Professor Wogglebug says it will, though I can't imagine why anyone would want to visit New York. I was there many times to participate in bowling matches. Although I had no brain then, I now can remember being very unhappy when I was in the United States. It isn't much fun doing nothing except roll down wooden alleys to knock over wooden pins, and to spend the rest of your life cooped up in the dark inside a bowling bag."

"Please tell us," said the Tin Woodman, "something about Ballville's history. How did you all get here?"

"Remember the Valley of Lost Things in Baum's *Dot and Tot in Merryland*?" the Mayor asked while he fastened a cloth napkin to the lower part of his body with a piece of tape.

Dorothy nodded. "It's where objects go after they've been lost for a long time."

"Precisely. Well, our town is like that. Whenever a ball on Earth or in Oz is lost, eventually it comes here. Don't ask me how or why. Nobody understands how or why things happen in Oz."

"But before you came here," said Dorothy, "you surely didn't have arms and legs and a brain. You weren't alive."

"True. But Oz magic is so strange and powerful that as soon as we arrive here we start to grow larger. We develop arms and legs, eyes and ears, internal organs, even a brain. Of course as soon as we grow a mind and a mouth we can talk to one another. We can pull our arms and legs into our body whenever we like to make our surface smooth. This allows us to roll along the ground whenever we want to go faster than our little legs can carry us."

To show what he meant, the Mayor drew in his arms and legs, and closed his eyes, ears, and mouth. The change was astonishing. He looked exactly like an ordinary bowling ball except for his larger size.

Mayor Ballard popped out his arms and legs, then opened his ears, eyes, and mouth. "Many of us have colorful histories. Take me for instance. I once belonged to Don Carter, a famous American bowler. They called him "Push-a-Ball" Carter because he had such an odd way of bowling. He would keep his right arm bent at right angles, place me on the alley, and give me a shove. I would roll slowly toward the pins, strike them, then they would all fall over."

"Did he lose you?" Dorothy asked.

"No. One of Carter's young fans, a boy of about seven, stole me. When he discovered I was too heavy for him, he dropped me into an ashcan and I got taken to a city dump. A few months later I ended up here."

"Let me tell *my* story," said a baseball sitting at a nearby table. He had a deep voice that was surprising coming from a person only a foot tall. "I was a home-run ball hit by the great Joe DiMaggio. He slammed me completely over the Yankee Stadium bleachers. No one ever found me."

A black pool ball with the number 8, sitting next to the baseball, had been listening. "I belonged to Minnesota Fats," he said.

"Me, too," said a red 7-ball at a table behind the 8-ball. "After Fats died, all fifteen of us ended up here."

Other balls in the room had similar stories to tell. A tennis ball had been played and discarded by Stefi Graf. A basketball had been owned by Magic Johnson. A golf ball, hit by Arnold Palmer, had landed in a lake where it stayed under water for almost a year before it was teleported to Ballville.

"I can recite 'Casey at the Bat,'" said the baseball. He hopped on top of his chair and began:

> *"The outlook wasn't brilliant for the Mudville nine that*
> * day;*
> *The score stood four to two with but one inning more to*
> * play.*

And then when Cooney died at first, and Barrows did
   the same,
A sickly silence fell upon the patrons of the game."

A football came over to the baseball's table, picked him up, and forced him back in his seat. "That's enough, Cooper. We've all heard you recite that ballad a hundred times."

"I haven't heard it before," said the tin man.

"Be glad you haven't," said the football. "Baseball is such a stupid sport. It's so slow moving. Not exciting like football."

"On the contrary," said Cooper. "It's football that's idiotic. Who cares to watch a bunch of burly men knock each other down just to get a funny looking ball over a goal line. Did I say *ball*? Why, you're not even round. You're a pinhead!"

"Now, now, you boys hush up, said the mayor, "or I'll have both of you thrown out of the room."

A red rubber ball drew in her arms and legs and began bouncing up and down on her chair. She bounced to the floor, then over and onto Dorothy's lap.

"My history is the most interesting of all," she said. "Martha Washington used me for playing jacks when she was little. Of course I was much smaller then. One day I bounced through an open window and into some shrubbery. Martha never could find me. As you see, even though I'm bigger now I'm as bouncy as ever." Everyone applauded as she bounced to the floor and back to her chair.

The Scarecrow was seated next to Miss Pong, a table-tennis ball with almond-shaped eyes. "Tell me," he asked, "do you people ever play games with balls?"

"Heavens no! When we were on Earth we got so battered that we developed an intense dislike of such games."

"You can't imagine how humiliating it is to be smashed over and over again by a heavy bat," said the baseball.

"Or viciously kicked thousands of times," chimed in a soccer ball.

"Of course we couldn't feel it at the time," added the baseball, "because we didn't have brains. But now we can remember all the times we got hit. Those memories are very painful."

"If you don't play with balls," asked the Scarecrow, "what kinds of games *do* you play?"

"We prefer intellectual games," said the soccer ball. "Games like chess and bridge."

"And Go," said a softball with a soft Japanese accent.

The Scarecrow stood up and started to leave.

"Oh, I didn't mean for *you* to go," said the softball. "Go is a board game that has been popular for centuries in Japan."

After lunch, which consisted mainly of spaghetti and meat balls, the Mayor arranged for his guests to be taken on a tour through what he called his ballutiful town. A friendly basketball was assigned as guide. She sat beside Dorothy on the Red Wagon's wide front bench to give instructions to the Sawhorse.

The Sawhorse was revolted by the sight of so many animated balls, but he kept his wooden mouth shut during the tour.

Dorothy and her friends greatly enjoyed the tour. They stopped many times to chat with residents, most of whom were astonished by the sight of a live scarecrow and a live tin man. They had unusual tales to tell about their experiences before coming to Ballville, though Dorothy never understood how they could remember anything about times when they had no brains. A highlight of the tour was a visit to the town's amusement park. It had a huge roller coaster ride, only instead of cars the balls rolled themselves around the looping track.

The Mayor invited the travelers to his home for supper. Mrs. Ballard, a large, jolly green bowling ball, served a delicious meal of matzo-ball soup, fish balls, and fresh peas. Dessert was half a cantaloupe with a ball of vanilla ice cream on top.

Dorothy assured the Mayor that she had a sleeping bag in the wagon and did not in the least mind spending the night outdoors, but the Mayor would have none of it. His large house, he said, had two guest rooms built especially for large outsiders.

Dorothy spent the night in one room while her friends occupied the other. Although neither the Scarecrow nor the Tin Woodman could sleep, the tin man was able to close his eyelids, and the straw man liked to relax with a towel over his painted eyes. Both men had learned how to go into a trance something like the trances of Buddhists and Hindus when they meditate.

Dorothy was so exhausted that she slept until it was almost nine. Mr. Ballard had already left for work. His rotund wife served Dorothy a tasty breakfast and gave her a large orange to eat on her ride back to the waterfall.

"Good-bye, friends," said Mrs. Ballard as she waved to Dorothy and her companions while they climbed into the Red Wagon. "Be careful not to hurt yourselves when you slide through that crazy bottle. I hope you all have a ball in New York."

On the way back to where they had left the Yellow Cart,

Dorothy tingled with excitement at the prospect of seeing her homeland after so many decades of living in Oz. Her companions, too, were eagerly anticipating the new adventure.

When they reached the clearing by the waterfall, the Sawhorse stopped abruptly with a cry of astonishment.

The Yellow Cart was still there but it was empty! The Klein Bottle was nowhere to be seen!

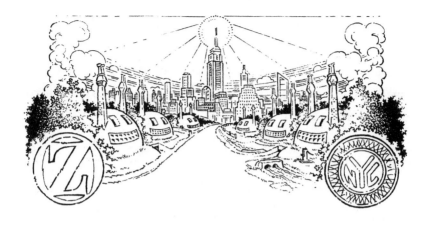

12

SHEERLUCK BROWN

SOMEONE OR some creature obviously had stolen the Klein Bottle.

During the night a steady drizzle of rain had turned the dirt road into mud. "Look!" shouted Dorothy as she pointed to the wet ground alongside the Yellow Cart.

In the dirt could be seen the shoeprints of a gigantic man!

The shoeprints continued past the Red Wagon and on down the road ahead. "If we follow these tracks," said the Scarecrow, "we may be able to reach the giant who stole our bottle."

"You don't say," snorted the Sawhorse. "You're supposed to

have superior brains, Scarecrow, but any fool could have fig-ured that out."

"Now, now," said the Tin Woodman. "We must try to be civil to one another. Let's track the shoeprints as Scarecrow suggests, and hope they end not too far away.

After reattaching the Yellow Cart to the back of the Red Wagon, the travelers climbed into the wagon and the Saw-horse began to trot slowly east along the road, following the trail of shoeprints. After going a few miles he paused when they came to a sign by the road. It said:

SHEERLUCK BROWN, THE ONLY
PRIVATE DETECTIVE IN OZ

"I never knew Oz had a private eye," said Dorothy. "But there are millions of things about Oz I don't know. Let's talk to Detective Brown. Maybe he can tell us who made those big shoeprints and where we can find the thief."

Dorothy and her companions climbed out of the Red Wagon to walk along a winding path that led to the entrance of a small brick house. A plaque above the door read 221B Butcher Street. The tin man rapped on the door with the handle of his axe.

A tall thin woman with a feather duster in one hand opened the door.

"We would like to see Mr. Brown," Dorothy said.

"Do you have an appointment?"

"No. We're travelers from the Emerald City. While we were asleep last night in Ballville someone stole something very valuable from a cart our wagon was pulling. We're hoping Mr. Brown can give us some advice on how to find the thief and get our possession back."

The woman glanced at the straw man and the tin man, but seemed not in the least surprised by their appearance. Most meat residents of Oz long ago learned not to be amazed by any kind of living creature, no matter how bizarre.

"Come in," the woman said. "You may wait in our living room while I tell Detective Brown you are here."

The woman left for a back room. As the travelers entered the living room they could hear strains of sad music being played on a violin. The music stopped, and the woman returned followed by a large brown bear. He was smoking a long curved pipe and wearing a deerstalker hat.

The bear took the pipe from his mouth, pointed its stem at Dorothy, and said, "You've not been in Gafanistan, I perceive."

"Gafanistan?" said the Scarecrow. "Where's that?"

"It's a mountain village east of here," replied Brown. "Please sit down. Mrs. Judson, my housekeeper, informs me that someone stole something of value from you last night."

The bear seated himself on a sofa, then knocked some glowing ashes from his pipe into a large purple ashtray on a glass side table. He placed his pipe alongside the ashtray. "I recognize the Scarecrow and the Tin Woodman," he said to Dorothy, "but who are you?"

"I'm Dorothy Gale."

The bear's eyebrows jumped up. "Not *the* Dorothy from Kansas—the Dorothy who destroyed the Wicked Witch of the West?"

"Yes, that's me," Dorothy responded with a smile as she

and her companions pulled over some chairs and sat down facing the sofa. "But before I tell you what happened, I'd like to know how you deduced I had never been to Gafanistan."

"Elementary, my dear young lady. Gafanistan is a most peculiar place. The natives are baboons who have three blue concentric circles in the hair on their backsides. Their eccentric ruler, Imbecileo, never allows visitors to leave until he tattoos three blue concentric circles on their forehead. The circles are permanent. There are no blue circles on *your* forehead. Therefore you have never been to Gafanistan."

"What a dreadful thing to do," said Dorothy. "Thanks for warning me. I'll make sure I never go there."

"A wise decision. The circles symbolize the three gods of a bizarre religion. Some visitors get trapped for life in Gafanistan and never escape."

The bear waved a paw toward his housekeeper, who had been standing silently nearby. "Thank you, Mrs. Judson. You may go now." The woman bowed slightly and left the room.

The bear turned toward the Scarecrow. "I perceive that you were stuffed with fresh straw before you left the Emerald City."

"True, true. And how, may I ask, did you deduce that?"

"As you can see, Scarecrow, I have a large and sensitive snout. I know well the smell of new-mown hay. I must say it's a very pleasant aroma."

"Thank you," said the straw man. "I couldn't agree more."

"I also perceive," Brown said to the tin man, "that your velvet heart is beating as strong and regularly as ever."

"It is indeed, but how could you tell?"

"Most elementary, Tin Man. As you can see, I have large and sensitive ears. Even from where I'm sitting I can hear your heart thumping with a steady beat."

Sheerluck leaned back on the sofa with his front paws touching each other and his eyes slightly closed. "Now kindly tell me all the details about your problem."

Dorothy described the Klein Bottle and explained how they planned to use it to enter the United States. The bear opened his eyes and wagged his head. "I have no idea how such a thing will get you to the earth, but I assume Professor Wogglebug understands it. I confess I know nothing about science or mathematics except when it relates directly to my work. I don't care a rap whether the earth goes around the sun or vice versa. You say there are large footprints in the muddy road?"

Dorothy nodded. "They are huge. Some giant must have stolen our bottle."

"Let's go have a look," said Brown.

Outside, the bear recognized the Red Wagon and the wooden animal hitched to it. "You must be the famous Sawhorse Ozma brought to life. I've heard a lot about you."

"Good things, I hope," said the Sawhorse. "I can't say I ever heard of *you*, but I'm pleased to meet you anyway."

Sheerluck, who was wearing shorts, got down on his bear knees, then took from a side pocket of his purple jacket a large magnifying glass. He examined the footprints carefully.

"Yes, I can identify these footprints. I've made a study, you know, of all the different kinds of shoeprints in Oz. My monograph on the topic is available in Professor Wogglebug's college library. Notice how the furrows on these footprints crisscross each other? They were made by shoes that belong to my neighbor Big Jim Foote. He's a friendly giant and a very decent chap. I'm surprised he would steal anything."

"How can we find him?" the tin man asked.

"Easy. Just keep following these shoeprints. You're lucky it rained last night or those prints wouldn't be here. When you come to a fork in the road, take the gravel road on the right. It leads straight to Big Jim's house. When you see him give him my regards. You can tell him that if he doesn't give your bottle back I'll have to report him to Captain Fyter. He's the tin soldier who polices the area."

"I know him well," remarked the Tin Woodman.

The bear got to his feet, scraped the mud off his bare knees, and returned the magnifying glass to his pocket. Dorothy thanked him profusely for his help.

"I'm always glad to be of some service to travelers," Detective Brown said, "especially to such distinguished ones. I hope you and your friends have a pleasant visit on Earth and that you get safely back to Oz."

The bear shook hands with everyone, then tipped his hat and walked back along the path to his house. At the entrance he turned to wave good-bye. Dorothy and her friends waved back as they climbed into the Red Wagon. Off they went, down the dirt road to look for Big Jim, and to see if they could get back the bottle he had taken.

13

—∿—

BIG JIM FOOTE

THE SAWHORSE trotted almost a mile before the footprints ended at a fork in the road. As instructed, he took
the gravel road on the right. It ended at a huge ramshackle
wooden farmhouse. There was the Klein Bottle, lying on its
side near the entrance, gleaming in the bright sunshine. Behind the house a giant about twenty feet tall, with a tangled
red beard and unruly red hair, had just pulled a large oak
tree out of the ground.

When the visitors left their wagon and walked toward him,
he tossed the tree aside. "I'm Big Jim Foote," he said. "Who
might ye be and what do ye want?"

"We want our bottle back," Dorothy answered.

"Well, you can't have it," said the giant. "Finders keepers. I found the thing. Now it's mine."

"No it isn't!" said Dorothy sternly. "It belongs to us. It's no use to you. Why did you steal it?"

"I know all about what it can do," said Big Jim. "My sister Kisma is the niece of Washa Foote, whose brother Smelly is a cousin of Ku-Klip. Kisma told me that if you drop anything into that thing it will land on a place called New York."

"But what good is that to you?" asked the Scarecrow.

"It will get rid of my trash and garbage, that's what. No one picks up trash around here. I have to carry it myself all the way to that forest over yonder and dump it. And that's a big pain in my foot. As you can see, by pulling up this tree I've made a big hole in the ground. I intend to bury the bottle here. Whenever I need to dispose of garbage, or get rid of anything else, I'll just dump it into that crazy bottle Ku-Klip made."

"Do you know anything about New York?" said Dorothy.

The giant shook his head. "Never heard of it. Must be a place somewhere under the ground."

Dorothy shuddered at the thought of garbage and other refuse, maybe even old rusty machinery, dropping onto Central Park.

"The bottle doesn't belong to you," said the tin man.

"It does now. I found it. It's mine. I don't know who this young woman is, but you must be the famous tin man who rules over the Winkies."

"I am," said the Tin Woodman with a slight bow. "And this is my friend Scarecrow. The girl is Dorothy Gale from Kansas."

"Well, I'll be gol' darned!" exclaimed Big Jim. "I'm pleased to meet ye. I don't know where Kansas is, but I've heard of Dorothy, and I should have recognized the Scarecrow."

"You should," said the straw man. "I'm just as well known as my tin friend. Will you give us back the bottle?"

"I will not! I know you didn't buy it from Ku-Klip, because money in Oz has been abolished. It's as much mine as yours." The giant thumped a finger on the bottle's side. It made the tin vibrate and produce a loud ringing sound.

"We'll see about that," said the tin man. "You may be stronger than any of us, but my axe is as sharp as a razor blade." He raised the axe then slammed it down on the tip of the giant's left shoe. It sliced off a tiny portion of leather.

"Let that be a warning," said the Tin Woodman as he twirled his axe the way a parade leader twirls a baton. "I can just as easily chop off one of your feet."

"You'll have to change your name," said the Sawhorse, "to Big Jim Onefoote."

"In fact," added the tin man, "I can chop you up into little pieces and drop them into that bottle." He shook his axe at the giant's belt. Of course the Tin Woodman was much too tenderhearted to do any such thing, but he guessed correctly that it would throw a scare into the giant.

Big Jim leaped back ten feet. "You almost cut off a toe!" he yelled. "I don't want to get into any fight."

"Then kindly put our bottle back on the Yellow Cart where you found it," said the tin man.

"All right, all right—if you insist," said Big Jim in a qua-vering voice. He picked up the bottle as easily as you or I can pick up a bottle of soda water, and set it on the cart. The tin ropes were still on the cart's floor where the giant had left them. He helped the Scarecrow and the Tin Woodman tie the bottle firmly back in place.

"That straw of yours," the giant said to the Scarecrow, "is not doing my hay fever any good." He reached into a pocket to pull out a handkerchief about the size of a tablecloth, but failed to get it to his nose in time. The sneeze was so mighty that it blew the Scarecrow off his feet, knocking him flat on his back.

Dorothy rushed, over. "Are you okay?"

"I'm fine," said the Scarecrow as he got back on his feet. "As you know, falls never injure me unless they rip my cloth and I lose some straw."

"Sorry about that, old chap," said the giant, as he wiped his nose. "Do you think that if I made a trip to Munchkin land and looked up Ku-Klip he could make another bottle for me?"

"No," said Dorothy. "I'll make sure Ku-Klip doesn't do any such thing. You don't seem to understand. Anything you drop into that bottle will fall on a beautiful park in New York City. It might even fall on the heads of people. We wouldn't want that to happen, would we?"

"I suppose not," said Big Jim. "I'm sorry I caused ye so much trouble. I'm not such a bad fellow when you get to know me."

"I think something's coming toward us through the sky," said the Tin Woodman.

Everybody looked up. Sure enough, a young woman was sailing overhead, holding tight to the handle of a large black umbrella. As she flew low over the giant's house she looked down, smiled, and said, "Good afternoon, Jim."

"Same to ye, Mary," said Big Jim as he took off his hat and waved it.

The woman, traveling rapidly over the treetops, became a small speck in the sky before she vanished from sight.

"Who in the world was that?" asked the Scarecrow.

"That was Mary Poppins," said the giant. "She lives a few miles north of here. Most of the time she stays home with her husband and ten children, but every now and then she flies off somewhere to work for a while as a nurse and nanny for parents who send for her."

"I've read about her," said Dorothy. "She used to visit families on Earth before Glinda moved Oz away. I wonder where she got that magic umbrella."

"I haven't the foggiest idea," said Big Jim, "but as long as I can remember, she's used it to take her wherever she wants to go."*

The giant turned toward Dorothy. "You must be starving, young lady. I assume your friends and that wooden horse never eat, but you surely do. My wife, Ophelia, will be glad to fix you a big sandwich to eat on your way back to Ballville."

---

* I later learned from a recently discovered notebook kept by the Royal Historian that Mary Poppins's magic umbrella was the same one that Button-Bright found in his attic, and which carried him, Trot, and Cap'n Bill to Sky Island. Oz buffs may recall that Button-Bright lost his umbrella while on a flight from his home in Philadelphia to Mo, an enchanted land adjacent to Oz.

According to Baum, Mary Poppins found the umbrella in a pile of popcorn snow while she was taking care of some Mo children. The umbrella's inventor is not known. The carved wooden head at the end of its handle keeps changing. For Button-Bright it was an elephant with beady red eyes. For Mary Poppins it most often is a talkative parrot.

"Thank you," said Dorothy, who had been wondering where her next meal would come from. Her wristwatch said two o'clock, and she was indeed hungry.

"You're right, I don't eat," said the Sawhorse to Big Jim. "But I have sharp teeth and I can bite. You're lucky I didn't bite a chunk out of your leg."

Ophelia Foote was a pleasant-looking giant, with a chubby freckled face, and almost as tall as her husband. At Jim's request she prepared a peanut-butter-and-jelly sandwich so large that on the ride back Dorothy could eat only a small portion.

"It was a pleasure to meet ye," Ophelia said as she watched the travelers climb into the Red Wagon.

"Have a nice day," added Big Jim.

The Sawhorse looked thoroughly disgusted but said nothing as he turned the wagon and cart around.

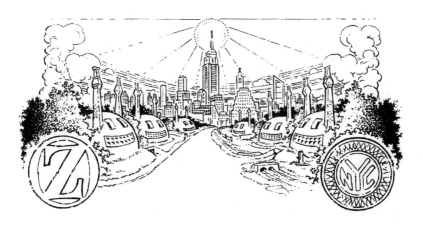

14

BACK TO BALLVILLE

AT THE clearing near the waterfall, the Scarecrow and Tin Woodman removed two shovels from the back of the Red Wagon and untied the Klein Bottle from the Yellow Cart. After digging a hole deep enough for the bottle's opening to be level with the ground, they lowered the bottle into the hole and packed loose dirt around it to keep it firmly in place.

For supper Dorothy ate another portion of the huge sandwich Ophelia Foote had given her, and added some food she had brought along in a paper sack. "I'm very thirsty," she said to the tin man. "Do you suppose the water in that waterfall is safe to drink?"

"We'll soon find out."

The Tin Woodman walked over to the waterfall where a stream of gold-tinted liquid was cascading over purple rocks to sparkle in the slanting light of a setting sun. He took off his funnel hat, then turned it upside down to make a cup. A hand over the funnel's spout kept the liquid from running out when he held the funnel under the falling water.

Dorothy was not in the least surprised to find that the "water" was apple cider. She had long ago learned not to find anything to be impossible in Oz.

As twilight came on and the western skies were turning pink and orange, a beach ball wearing a polka-dotted bikini rolled into the clearing. She was followed by a male croquet ball with a blue belt around his middle. The two had heard about the Klein Bottle and were curious to see what it looked like.

The beach girl rolled over to the bottle's edge so she could peer down into the dark interior. The croquet ball, an irresponsible, mischievous chap, rolled toward her and knocked her into the opening. In his past life, if you can call it a life, he had been so accustomed to knocking croquet balls out of the court that this was a temptation he couldn't resist.

Down below, in Central Park, the beach ball bounced off the head of a man in shorts who was jogging around the park's reservoir. He rubbed the top of his head and looked startled.

"Sorry about that," said the beach ball, looking up from the ground. "I didn't intend to hit you."

"I must be going nuts," the jogger said to himself. "What will my psychiatrist think if I tell her I heard a beach ball talk?"

He gave the ball a mighty kick that sent it soaring over the reservoir's wire fence. She landed in the water with a splash, then floated to the center of the artificial lake. The kick had knocked her unconscious. No longer in Oz, her arms and legs began to shrivel and vanish. Her brains soon disappeared. Several days later, a small boy found the ball drifting along the reservoir's edge. He picked it up and took it home. Who knows? Years later it may go back to Ballville to be revived and given a second life in Oz.

Dorothy was furious with the croquet ball. She picked him up, and even though he was larger and heavier than in his previous "life," she was able to heave him down the road that led to Ballville. After landing on the dirt with a loud thump, he turned around to giggle and thumb his nose before he pulled in his arms and legs to begin a rapid roll back to town.

While the Scarecrow and the Tin Woodman were digging the hole, Ozma had been observing them in her Magic Picture. She correctly assumed that at ten the next morning the travelers would be entering the bottle. She phoned Glinda, who in turn sent Samuel Gold an E-mail letter telling him to be at a certain spot in Central Park, near the reservoir, at three A.M. the following morning.

A few minutes later, back came an E-mail message from Gold's secretary saying he would be there. Professor Wogglebug had determined that New York Time was seven hours earlier than time in Oz. Everyone agreed that three A.M. was the best hour for the travelers to arrive because there would then be few people, if any, in the park to see the travelers drop suddenly on the grass.

As darkness came on, Dorothy removed her suitcase and sleeping bag from the Red Wagon. The shovels were taken to a side of the clearing where they could be hidden under some bushes. They would be needed later on when the travelers returned to Oz, and they would have to remove the bottle from the ground.

"Do you suppose Big Jim will come back here and steal the bottle again?" the Scarecrow asked Dorothy.

"I doubt it. He'll be afraid the Tin Woodman might return to his house and chop off his leg."

"If he does try to steal it again," observed the Sawhorse, "he wouldn't need the shovels. He could yank that bottle out of the ground with one hand."

"True," said the Tin Woodman. "But it was good to hide the shovels so no one else coming along the road will be tempted to take them."

"I assume you won't need me anymore," said the Sawhorse to Dorothy. "That is, unless you want me to hang around to make sure you get safely through the bottle."

"That won't be necessary, Sawhorse. Ozma will be watching us in her Magic Picture. I'm sure she'll be able to take care of us if there's any emergency. I know you don't mind traveling at night. You can leave now if you like. We're very grateful to you for bringing us here and for being such a good and obedient horse."

"Don't mention it. I can't say I enjoyed either the trip to see Ku-Klip or the trip here. Talking balls are an abomination. Mount Olympus and Wonderland might have been more interesting, but you wouldn't let me come along on those two visits."

"Sorry about that," said Dorothy. "I should have asked if you wanted to join us, though I doubt you would have liked either place."

"You're probably right. To tell you the truth, Dorothy, I don't much care for bizarre places. The Emerald City is weird enough, but at least I can enjoy friendships there with the Cowardly Lion and the Hungry Tiger."

"Don't forget Toto."

"Yes, of course. Toto's another good pal. We animals, you know, get along much better among ourselves than with humans and gods, or with talking eggs, playing cards, chess pieces, and balls. Inanimate objects shouldn't be alive."

"How about wooden sawhorses?" asked the Scarecrow. He felt insulted by the Sawhorse's remark.

"I admit I'm no exception. Nobody asked me if I wanted to be alive. However, now that I am, I suppose I should feel grateful."

"Speaking of animals," said Dorothy, "let me remind you that outside of Oz wild beasts are not so kind to one another. I admit that a hungry tiger on Earth would have trouble trying to eat you, but an elephant could pick you up with his trunk and dash you to splinters. Anyway, we're all glad you're alive, Sawhorse, and we enjoyed having you along. Ozma couldn't do without you. I expect we'll be seeing you again when we return to this spot."

"Assuming that bottle works in both directions," said the Sawhorse.

"Professor Wogglebug says it will."

"Well, I hope the old bug's right. So long. Have a good trip."

It was a quiet night. All you could hear was the sound of the nearby waterfall. The sky was splattered with those monstrous balls of fire we call stars, although their patterns were not the same as those seen from Earth. There was no Big

Dipper or Orion. A large constellation that Ozians call the Camel was rising in the east.

The Sawhorse waved good-bye with a front leg, then broke into a fast gallop as he drove off into the night, taking the empty wagon and cart back to the Emerald City.

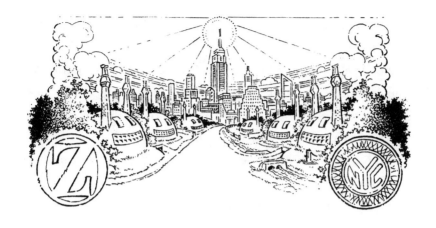

15

NEW YORK

A CLOUDY sky kept the rising sun from awakening Dorothy until late in the morning. She slipped her left arm out of her sleeping bag to check the time on her wristwatch. It was almost nine.

The Scarecrow had discovered near the waterfall some bushes laden with large purple berries. He brought one to Dorothy who said it tasted something like a juicy apricot. It was so delicious that she ate six for breakfast, then finished what was left of Ophelia Foote's big sandwich. The Tin Woodman brought her another cup of apple cider in his upside-down funnel hat.

"Shall we take your sleeping bag with us?" the straw man asked Dorothy.

"No. We'll leave it here by the entrance to the bottle. Mr. Gold has offered to let us stay in his apartment. I may need the bag, though, when we get back to Ballville."

"Aren't you afraid someone might steal it?"

"They might. If they do, I don't much mind. It's old and worn, and falling apart."

At exactly ten, the time in Oz when it would be three A.M. in New York, Dorothy lowered herself into the bottle, holding fast to its curved rim before she let go. It felt like coasting down what in Kansas, as a child, she called a chute-the-chute. A moment later she dropped out of the bottle's tube to land on her feet in the grass alongside the path that circles the Central Park Reservoir.

The Scarecrow went next, carrying Dorothy's suitcase. He emerged from the tube with a *whoosh* to land on his back without letting go of the suitcase. While Dorothy was helping him to his feet, a clanking sound was heard overhead as the tin man, carrying his axe, dropped down beside them.

"That was much easier than I anticipated," he said. "But where's Mr. Gold?"

It was dark in Central Park, although an almost full moon, high in the sky, was casting a silver light over the lawns and trees. Knowing Ozma would be watching with her Magic Picture, Dorothy raised her right hand to make a circle with her thumb and first finger. It let Ozma know that all had gone well—that she and her friends were now safely in New York.

Samuel Gold was standing not far away, unsure of the precise spot where the visitors would land. As soon as he saw them, he ran as fast as he could to greet them. He was so

overcome with emotion at seeing Dorothy in the flesh, and
her companions in straw and tin, that he could hardly speak.
Yes, it was really them! Wow! They looked exactly like the
pictures by John R. Neill, the Royal Illustrator of Oz—pictures Sammy had so loved as a boy. And here were all three,
in Manhattan, just as he had hoped and planned!

Gold finally regained enough composure to stammer:
"It's . . . it's only a short walk to my apartment. At this hour
I doubt if we'll meet anyone along the way. Here, let me
carry that suitcase."

Sammy was right. Not a soul could be seen, although a
stray cat and a gray squirrel scurried off into the shadows
when they caught sight of the travelers.

At the eastern edge of the park a dog that seemed to belong
to nobody trotted over to the tin man to sniff his feet. They
didn't smell human. Mystified by the oily odor, the dog began
to growl and bare its teeth. Suddenly it bit the tin man's calf.

The Tin Woodman was tempted to swing his axe at the
dog before he remembered that his kind heart would never
allow him to harm the poor beast. In any case, frightening
off the dog wasn't necessary. The bite had broken one of its
teeth. The dog ran off yelping with pain.

Gold's Fifth Avenue apartment was huge and richly fur-
nished. Paintings on the wall puzzled the Scarecrow and Tin
Woodman because they seemed to be totally meaningless.
They didn't resemble anything.

"Toto could do better than that with his tail," said the tin
man as he examined a painting signed "Jackson Pollock."

Dorothy's room had a king-size bed and a large bathroom
with a Jacuzzi. "You'll be needing new clothes," said Sammy
as he showed her the room. "As soon as I know your size, I'll

see that some fine dresses and other clothing—even some new shoes—are bought and put in your closet. I'll leave now while you freshen up. Have you had breakfast?"

Dorothy nodded. "I ate some fruit and part of a sandwich. I would, though, enjoy a cup of hot coffee."

"Coffee coming up," said Gold as he left to go to the kitchen.

Later, while she and Sammy sipped coffee in a breakfast nook, Dorothy said, "You must be very sleepy. *I'm* wide awake because for me it's late morning. But you had to get up in the middle of the night to meet us."

"I'm much too excited to go back to sleep," Sammy replied as he refilled his coffee cup for the third time. "I've got a thousand questions to ask you about Oz. Have you seen the MGM movie in which Judy Garland, bless her soul, played you?"

Dorothy shook her head. "Everyone in Oz knows about that film, but I don't think anyone has actually seen it."

"Well, you and your friends will be seeing it this evening."

The Scarecrow and Tin Woodman shared a room across the hall from Dorothy's bedroom. After Sammy and Dorothy finished their coffee, her friends joined them in the living room. You can imagine the conversation that took place during the next three hours. Sammy asked question after question. Dorothy and her companions did their best to answer, while Sammy scribbled endless notes on a large pad of yellow paper.

Gold's wife had remained at their home in Beverly Hills, California. Their children, as mentioned before, were off at a summer camp in Minnesota. A Spanish cook and housekeeper named Molly Sanchez came to Gold's apartment every morning except Tuesday, her day off. When she arrived at seven-thirty (two-thirty in the afternoon by Dorothy's watch), Dorothy was hungry enough to devour a hearty breakfast. The sun had risen. Through the apartment's open windows, one could see and hear the cars and buses rolling down Fifth Avenue.

Molly was so frightened when she first saw the Scarecrow and Tin Woodman that she opened her mouth to scream, then quickly made a sign of the cross over her heart. As the day progressed she managed to keep calm. Mr. Gold had tried to prepare her for the strangers, but she didn't really believe him until she actually saw them. Eventually she was able to behave as if the two men were ordinary flesh and blood.

Gold had notified the city's newspapers and television stations that he would hold a press conference in his apartment at ten that morning. Before the reporters arrived, he discussed in detail with Dorothy and her friends how they should act and reply to questions.

"No one will believe you're really from Oz," Sammy said, "but don't let that upset you. Just answer the questions honestly and as best you can. We'll soon find out how the reporters will react."

Dorothy twisted her watch hands backward to New York time. By ten the apartment was jammed with reporters, photographers, and TV camera crews, all eager to see the visitors Gold claimed had come directly from Oz. As Sammy had predicted, not a person in the crowd believed this. They took for granted it was a fiendishly clever flimflam Gold had dreamed up to publicize his plans for a new Oz musical.

Dorothy was real enough, but the Scarecrow and tin man greatly puzzled the reporters. They were convinced that the straw man was someone inside a cloth costume, like Ray Bolger in the MGM film. The tin man's arms and legs, however, were much too thin to conceal human limbs. The reporters decided he was some sort of robot ingeniously animated and electronically controlled by a person concealed in another room, perhaps watching through a peephole? But they were flabbergasted by how genuine both men appeared. Each spoke with a slight accent. It was an accent the listeners had never heard before.

As for Dorothy, they assumed she was just a young and attractive teenage actress Gold had hired for the occasion. Did he intend, they wondered, to feature her in his forthcoming film? The conference was such great fun that the reporters pretended to believe everything the visitors said. In their opinion it was the greatest hoax ever perpetrated to publicize a movie.

After Gold finished his opening remarks, he introduced the three visitors. They had agreed, he said, to talk about their life in Oz and to answer questions.

The Scarecrow was the first to stand. He spoke of how Dorothy had found him hanging in a cornfield alongside the Yellow Brick Road, just as Baum described in his first Oz book. He told how he had joined Dorothy and Toto on their way to see the Wizard. The reporters noticed that when the Scarecrow talked his painted mouth never moved. This strengthened their belief that he was an actor speaking through a cloth mask.

The Tin Woodman stood up next to tell how a wicked witch had enchanted his axe, causing it to chop him into pieces, and how Ku-Klip the Tinsmith used magic glue to replace each severed part with tin until he was all tin. He spoke of how he had rusted in a forest until Dorothy rescued him by oiling his arm and leg joints and his jaws. Then he, too, had joined Dorothy, the Scarecrow, and Toto on their journey to the Emerald City. The best account of his later life, he said, was in Baum's *The Tin Woodman of Oz*. Of course no one in the audience believed a word he said.

"Why didn't the Cowardly Lion come with you?" Gina Kolata, *The New York Times* science editor, asked. She could hardly keep from laughing at her question because it sounded as if she really thought Dorothy had come from Oz.

Dorothy didn't smile. She carefully explained that the lion knew he would be unable to talk outside Oz. Besides, he was fearful of being captured and locked up in some dreadful zoo.

Dorothy then arose and gave an account of her own history—how she had been raised an orphan on a dreary farm in Kansas, and lived there until 1900 when a tornado lifted her house and carried her and Toto to the Munchkin country of Oz. She spoke of how she got home by using the magic slippers, and about her later trips to Oz until she finally decided to live there forever. She told how Ozma had used her Magic Belt to teleport Uncle Henry and Aunt Em from their farm to join her in the Emerald City.

"You say you first entered Oz in 1900," said Margaret Carlson, a reporter from *Time*. "How could that be? You obviously are not over a hundred years old."

"I decided to stop growing when I was seventeen," Dorothy replied with a smile. "Persons in Oz can stop getting old whenever they like. No one can age beyond seventy. And no one ever dies from natural causes."

Carlson nodded and grinned while she jotted down Dorothy's remarks. "Can you tell us how you and your friends got to New York?"

Dorothy tried to explain how Glinda, many decades ago, had moved Oz to a parallel universe, and how they managed to cross a few feet of the fourth dimension to get to New York by way of a curious topological structure called a Klein Bottle. Her explanation of all this caused much shaking of heads and frequent chuckling. Flash bulbs constantly popped around the room. The TV cameras never stopped whirring to catch every word.

The conference was a smashing success. It made the front page of every newspaper in the New York City area, and was the lead story that night on every television news show. The wire services sent out long releases that ran on the first page of hundreds of newspapers both in the United States and abroad.

The media decided to play along with what they considered a swindle that far outrivaled anything P. T. Barnum could have imagined. Pictures of the visitors from Oz appeared simultaneously on the covers of *Time, Newsweek,* and *U.S. News & World Report.* Even *The Wall Street Journal* carried a front-page account of the conference. It predicted correctly that toy and department stores would soon be jammed with replicas of the Scarecrow and Tin Woodman. There was a straw man whose brains lit up when you pushed a button at the back of his head, and a tin man with a battery that made him walk and produced the sound of a beating heart when you put an ear to his chest.

The weekly supermarket tabloids also had great sport with news of the supposed Oz visitors. *The National Enquirer* offered Dorothy fifty thousand dollars to reveal who was dressed like the Scarecrow and how the metal robot operated. A *New York Times* editorial, headed ALIENS FROM HYPERSPACE, congratulated Samuel Gold on having concocted the greatest and funniest hoax of the twentieth century.

Only *The Washington Post* was not amused. It asserted on its editorial page that Gold's "Ozgate" was exploiting the superstitions of American children. It's bad enough, said an anonymous writer, that so many youngsters today believe in witches, angels, demons, vampires, ghosts, and extraterrestrials visiting Earth in flying saucers. The writer accused Gold of adding to the "dumbing down" of American youth by suggesting that the whimsical creatures of the Oz books were also real.

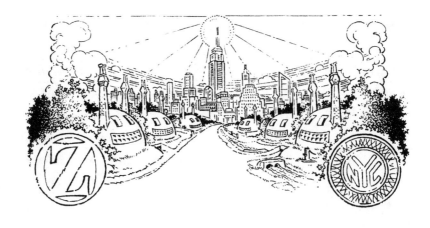

16

BUFFALO BOGGS

A FTER THE press conference, Dorothy took her friends on a stroll through Central Park. They were followed by throngs of New Yorkers, astonished by what they were seeing. Reporters kept popping questions.

At the famous statue of Alice, Dorothy obliged a cameraman by climbing into Alice's lap for pictures that showed her surrounded by bronze replicas of the Mad Hatter, the White Rabbit, and the Dormouse. The Scarecrow and Tin Woodman stood alongside her.

Dorothy tried to convince the reporters that Wonderland was a real place below ground in the Gillikin region of Oz. "We visited there last week. Lewis Carroll made lots of mis-

takes when he wrote about Alice's dream visits. If you like, I can tell you some of them."

Of course the reporters refused to believe her, but they were so fascinated by everything Dorothy said that her remarks were quoted in every New York newspaper.

That evening, in his apartment, Samuel Gold took his guests to a back room where he projected MGM's *Wizard of Oz* on a large screen. Dorothy's companions were charmed by Judy Garland's portrayal of Dorothy. They laughed heartily at Ray Bolger's wobbly dancing, at Jack Haley's antics as the tin man, and especially at Bert Lahr's outrageous clowning as the Cowardly Lion. Dorothy loved the way the film opened with colorless Kansas scenery, then burst into brilliant colors when she walked out of her house and said to Toto, "I have a feeling we're not in Kansas anymore."

"That's *exactly* how it was," Dorothy remarked.

All four agreed that Billie Burke was sadly miscast as Glinda. "Glinda's so much younger," said Dorothy, "and she never speaks in such a silly voice. Frank Morgan made the Wizard act like an idiot. He's really a very intelligent and kind man. And I couldn't stand that midget who sings about the lollipop kids. There are no lollipop kids in Oz. What a stupid song! Why in the world did the director think it worth adding to the film?"

Everyone was outraged by the movie's ending. "Whatever made the writers think Oz was just my dream?" Dorothy wanted to know.

"I couldn't agree more," said Sammy. "It completely destroyed the picture's wonderful mood. I promise you *my* musical won't turn out to be a dream."

Now, patient reader, I regret to inform you that while Gold

was getting such great publicity for his forthcoming film, something ominous was taking place in Hollywood. You will recall from our first chapter that Gold's top rival and bitter enemy was Buffalo Odersby Boggs. He, too, was planning a blockbuster fantasy that would use computer graphics. It was to be, remember, a new musical version of Peter Pan, starring Madonna as a singing and dancing Peter.

Buffalo was fit to be tied over the the way the media ignored his plans. Why were they ignored? Because Samuel Gold was grabbing all the media's attention with his phony visitors from Oz.

There was only one way, Boggs decided, to put a stop to Gold's publicity blitz. As I mentioned earlier, Buffalo had strong connections with New York City's criminal underworld. Two brawny brothers known as Mugsy and Bugsy were notorious hit men Boggs had used before to harass his competitors.

Mugsy and Bugsy were identical twins. When they were born in Brooklyn, New York, even their mother was unable to tell them apart. Like Tweedledum and Tweedledee, they were mirror images of each other. Mugsy parted his hair on the right, Bugsy on the left. Both had crooked smiles. When Mugsy smiled, only the left side of his mouth curled up and he squinted his left eye. Bugsy's smile and squint were on the other side. Their fingerprints in FBI files were almost impossible to tell apart. I do not know if their hearts were on opposite sides.

Boggs invited the twin felons to his studio. "How much will it cost me," he asked, "if I hire you to destroy those two bums who pretend to be the Scarecrow and Tin Woodman?"

Bugsy squinted while he rubbed the dark stubble on his chin. For several minutes he and his brother conversed in such low tones that Buffalo couldn't make out what they were saying.

"We'll do the job for ten thousand to each of us," Mugsy finally announced.

Boggs grinned while he unbent a paper clip and used it to pick his left ear. He sniffed the point before he tossed the clip into a wastebasket. He had expected the twins to name twice that amount. "It's a done deal," he said as he shook their hands.

Back in Manhattan, Dorothy and her friends were guests on Oprah Winfrey's talk show. Like everyone else, Oprah could not believe the two men were genuine. She reached behind a desk to produce a harpoon of the sort used for spearing whales.

"If you really are what you say you are," she said to the straw man, "will you allow me to run this harpoon through your body?"

"Certainly."

The Scarecrow's willingness caught Miss Winfrey by surprise. She quickly backed down, fearful that the harpoon would kill whoever was inside the cloth costume. And that would be a terrible thing to happen live on her show.

"I perceive you hesitate," said the Scarecrow as he took the harpoon from Oprah's hand. "If you're unwilling to spear me, let me do it myself."

The straw man stood up from his chair, placed the harpoon's point against his belly, then rammed it all the way through his body. You could hear the gasps of Oprah and her audience. The Scarecrow turned around to show the harpoon projecting behind his back.

Oprah's mouth was open wide. She put a hand on her chest.

"It must be a trick," she mumbled. "I remember seeing David Copperfield do something like that on one of his TV magic spectaculars."

"No, it's not an illusion," said the Scarecrow as he pulled the harpoon out of his body and handed it back to Miss Winfrey. He took a roll of cloth tape from a pocket and used a piece to patch the hole in his abdomen. He asked Dorothy to patch the hole on his back.

"Those patches are just temporary," Dorothy said, "to keep my friend's straw from poking out. I'll sew the holes together as soon I get a chance."

The Tin Woodman stood up and put aside his axe. "I suppose you think I, too, am a fake," he said to Oprah. He opened the small door on his chest. Oprah and her viewers could clearly see a large red silk heart slowly throbbing.

"The Wizard gave me this beautiful heart," the tin man said proudly. "If you look inside me you'll observe there are no wires or machinery. I'm just what you see—a real live hollow man made entirely of high-quality nickel-plated tin."

Oprah was still too dazed to speak.

Dorothy, who had been watching Oprah's reactions with amusement, broke the silence by picking up from beside her chair a saw she had asked Oprah to obtain for her. "When I was a a girl in Kansas, one of our farm hands taught me how to play this thing." She reached down again to pick up a cello bow.

"While I play the saw," she continued, "Scarecrow will favor us with a song. He has a fine tenor voice."

Dorothy gripped the saw's wooden handle between her knees. With her left hand at the end of the saw, she bent the blade into the shape of an elongated S. With her right hand she drew the bow across the saw's smooth edge—an edge heavily coated with rosin. The result was a strong clear musical note.

Dorothy gave the tone a vibrato by jiggling one leg up and down. Then she began to play a lively tune popular in Oz called "The Winkie Polka," while the Scarecrow stood and sang the lyrics:

> *Throw away all your heartaches.*
> *Shout out good-bye to your woes.*
> *Now's the time to laugh and be happy*
> *From your head to the tips of your toes.*
>
> *Give a big kiss to your partner.*
> *Enjoy yourself the whole night long,*
> *While you dance the Winkie Polka*
> *And I belt out this song!*

The Tin Woodman supplied a rhythmic drumbeat by banging his fists on his hollow chest.

As you can imagine, the three visitors from Oz were in constant demand as guests on other TV talk shows. On *Geraldo Live* the Scarecrow wowed the studio audience by sticking a darning needle through his head. The Tin Woodman performed a juggling routine with his axe, twirling it around his hands, over his neck, and under his legs, while Dorothy played "Turkey in the Straw" on the saw, which Oprah had allowed her to keep. The tin man finished by balancing his axe on the tip of his long nose.

"I assure you there is no turkey in my straw," quipped the Scarecrow.

For the rest of the show the three visitors answered questions from home viewers who telephoned Geraldo.

"How are you able to talk without moving your lips?" a woman asked.

"I'm a ventriloquist," the straw man answered, then quickly added, "Seriously, I really don't know. Oz is a place of endless mystery. I'm one of its miracles. My tin friend here is another. We long ago learned to accept such wonders and not worry about how or why they happen."

"Have you ever thought of getting married?" another woman wanted to know.

"No. However, the Patchwork Girl and I are dear friends. We might consider it some day."

"How about you?" The caller directed his question to the Tin Woodman.

"I was once engaged to a beautiful Munchkin girl, but it didn't work out. She's married now to a meat person. If I met a tin woman I liked, I suppose I might consider marriage, even though my heart is not a loving one. I must say, however, that in Oz we persons not made of flesh and blood seldom consider marriage."

Dorothy answered the same question by saying that she often thought of marrying and having children, but was waiting for the right man to come along. "I have several boyfriends," she added, but she refused to identify them.

For the next two weeks Dorothy and her companions appeared on almost every other major talk show around the country. Samuel Gold owned a private plane that took them wherever they needed to go. Newspapers and magazines were filled with articles speculating about the identity of the man inside the straw man's costume. Theories abounded on the

Internet about how the tin robot was controlled by someone nearby or perhaps by a midget inside his hollow body.

Sales of Oz books by Baum and others skyrocketed. Pat Robertson and several other televangelists denounced the Scarecrow and Tin Woodman as being forms assumed by Satan's demons. The magician and skeptic James Randi invited the two men to come to his laboratory in Fort Lauderdale, Florida, for scientific testing to determine whether they were what they claimed to be. They were too busy, however, to accept his invitation.

New York City's mayor Rudolph Giuliani was so amused and impressed by what he called the greatest publicity hoax of all time that he invited Dorothy and her friends to City Hall, where he presented each with a key to the city. One of his assistants, dressed like the Cowardly Lion, carried the silver keys to the Mayor on a plush green cushion.

"We are deeply honored," Giuliani said, "to welcome such distinguished visitors to our fair city. Of course, the Big Apple can't compare with the beauty and splendor of the Emerald City, but at least we have here a Mayor who isn't a humbug like that wizard from Omaha who ruled Oz before Princess Ozma was restored to the throne."

The ceremony was covered by all the major television news programs. Dorothy gave a brief but charming speech after she accepted her key. She reminded the Mayor that her old friend the Wizard was no longer a humbug, but a skillful sorcerer who learned Oz magic from Glinda. The Tin Woodman drew gasps from the audience when he opened the door on his chest so everyone could see his beating red heart. The Scarecrow wowed the crowd by singing a popular Oz song, followed by a comic dance in imitation of Ray Bolger.

One afternoon, when Dorothy took her friends to the observation deck on the eighty-sixth floor of the Empire State Building, Mugsy and Bugsy followed them on the next elevator. The brothers had been trailing them for weeks, waiting for a good opportunity to kill the Scarecrow and the Tin Woodman. They waited patiently until no other tourists were on the deck.

The Scarecrow was admiring the tall towers of the city when Mugsy darted forward, picked him up—he was astonished by how little the straw man weighed—and flung him over the railing.

Dorothy screamed. She and the tin man, followed by Bugsy, rushed to the railing. Bugsy's eyes bugged out when he saw the Scarecrow pick himself up from the sidewalk and wave up at Dorothy. His fall naturally attracted a large crowd of passersby. They clustered around him in amazement, and looked up, trying to see what had happened on the building's observation deck.

Dorothy turned around and screamed again when she saw Mugsy whip out a revolver and fire it six times at the Tin Woodman. Because his nickel-plated body was harder than the hardest steel, the bullets bounced off his chest without even leaving dents.

The tin man said not a word. He just raised his axe and walked slowly toward the brothers. They turned and fled. Not waiting for an elevator, they dashed to the stairway entrance and ran all the way down eighty-six floors to the bottom.

Dorothy and the Tin Woodman took the next elevator down to rejoin the Scarecrow. You might suppose they would be mobbed by New Yorkers wanting to speak to them and get their autographs. But New Yorkers are a jaded breed, long accustomed to seeing strange characters walk the streets. Having read all about the visitors from Oz, and having seen them on television, they did little more than smile, wag their heads in wonder, and walk on.

A police car, its sirens blaring, drew up to the curb. Two officers jumped out and quickly dispersed the crowd. Dorothy and her companions managed to slip away before the police could question them. Mayor Giuliani arrived on the scene too late to be photographed with the miraculously uninjured Scarecrow.

Boggs was outraged when the brothers phoned to tell him how their plans had failed. He at once flew to New York in his private jet for a conference with the two hit men. The three met in a basement bar in Little Italy—a bar that is a popular hangout for the city's mobsters.

"I know you won't believe it," said Mugsy, "but that straw man really *is* made of straw. And that tin man really *is* made of tin. His body stops bullets like Superman. I can't understand it. I must be going bats."

"You must be," agreed Boggs. "Any fool knows those two creeps are fakes, even though nobody seems to understand how that metal robot operates. If you can't destroy 'em, surely you can get rid of the girl. I'll triple what I offered. Forget about her funny friends, at least for now. We can dispose of them later. Meanwhile, take care of the girl."

Boggs took another swallow of beer, then wiped his mouth with the back of his hand. "My spies tell me that the girl, whoever she is, likes to get up early and jog around the reservoir in Central Park. I don't mind how you kill her. Just *do* it!"

"I'll see it gets done tomorrow morning, boss," Mugsy replied with a lopsided grin. "You can depend on it."

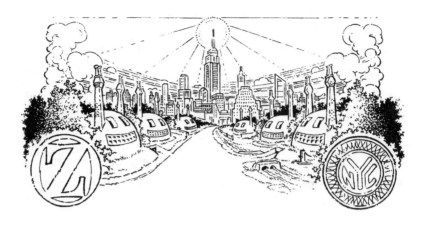

17

DOROTHY USES HER RING

SAMUEL GOLD was horrified when Dorothy told him
what had happened on top of the Empire State Building.
"I suspect my old enemy Buffalo Boggs hired those men.
Would you like me to give you a bodyguard?

Dorothy shook her head. "I don't think that will be necessary, Mr. Gold. "I'm more worried about my friends. Those
two ruffians didn't try to harm *me*. It was the Scarecrow and
Tin Woodman they tried to kill."

Dorothy was tempted to tell Gold about the enchanted
pearls in the tips of her shoes, and about the emerald ring
she wore, but she decided it was best, at least for now, not to
mention them.

"Perhaps I should hire a bodyguard for your two friends."

"Not a bad idea," said Dorothy.

The next morning, bright and early, Dorothy had no ink-ling of what was in store for her when she started to jog around the reservoir. Mugsy was there alone, hiding behind a bush near the path. It was so early in the morning that the grass was still wet with dew, and the path was deserted of other runners.

As Dorothy was rounding a curve, Mugsy leaped from behind the bush with a large knife in his hand. Dorothy stopped running when she saw him blocking her path.

Mugsy noticed the emerald ring on Dorothy's hand. "If that ring isn't a fake," he thought, "I can sell it for lots of money. Besides, taking it will make it look as if the girl was killed by a thief."

In a low menacing voice Mugsy said: "Hand over that ring, young lady, unless you want me to slash that pretty throat of yours."

Dorothy held back a scream. She knew the pink pearl would protect her, but she decided to press the emerald in case she needed additional help. To give Ozma time to get to the Magic Picture, she pretended she couldn't get the ring off her finger.

"So it's you again," she said. "You're one of the men who tried to kill my friends yesterday."

"How perceptive," snarled Mugsy.

He suddenly noticed that the ring's jewel had changed color. "I swear, I thought that stone was green. Now it looks red!"

"It's a magic ring," Dorothy said, still stalling for time. "It changes color whenever I'm in trouble."

"Oh, yeah? Well, magic or not, let's have it. Hand it over, sister, and be quick about it. If you can't get it off I'll cut off your finger and get it that way."

Ozma was having lunch when the chiming of her emerald ring, now glowing bright red, startled her. She leaped to her feet, grabbed her wand from the dresser, and rushed to the Magic Picture. In an instant the tense scene in Central Park was before her.

Ozma wasted no time. She took her Magic Belt from the peg where it was hanging next to the Magic Picture, and fastened it around her waist. She pressed the emerald on her ring. Then she raised her wand and moved it in figure-eight circles while she spoke some strange words Glinda had taught her.

Dorothy's ring began to chime. The knife in Mugsy's hand suddenly flew out of his grasp and ended up in Dorothy's right hand.

"Now," said Dorothy with a grim smile, her blue eyes flashing, "it's *my* turn to cut *your* throat!"

Mugsy backed away, his eyes wide with terror. A large rock at the edge of the path sent him sprawling. He struggled to his feet, then turned and ran as fast as he could. As he ran, the knife left Dorothy's hand and followed close behind him. It kept jabbing him in the rear.

"Ouch! Ooch! Ouch!" Mugsy shouted with each jab.

The enchanted knife, obedient to Ozma's thoughts as she watched the scene in her Magic Picture, tipped its point upward and neatly sliced the back of Mugsy's belt. Trying hard to keep his pants up with both hands, Mugsy vanished over a hill and out of Dorothy's sight.

The knife returned to Dorothy's hand. While she was wondering what to do with it, it slowly faded away.

Assuming Ozma was still watching, Dorothy raised a hand to give the V-sign of victory. She formed a silent "thank you" with her lips, then blew Ozma a kiss.

Dorothy returned to Gold's apartment after she finished her jog around the reservoir. When she took off her left sneaker—the shoes were part of her new wardrobe—she wondered if the pink pearl would be gone. No, it was still here. Somehow it must have known, she reasoned, that Ozma had full control of the situation.

Still shaken from her narrow escape, Dorothy was greatly relieved to see the pink pearl. She was well aware that outside of Oz it was possible she could be killed. What if Ozma had not been in her palace when her ring chimed? Would the pink pearl alone have been powerful enough to stop the man from trying to murder her?

Dorothy wondered what the pink pearl would have done. She realized, with a shiver, that she might need its protection on yet another occasion before her sojourn on Earth was over.

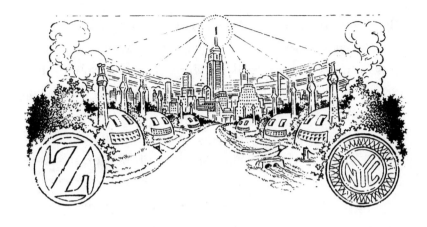

18

HIJACK!

FOR THOSE too young to remember, Dorothy had been seven in 1900 when a tornado in Kansas blew her and Toto to Oz. The magic of the witch's silver slippers (ruby slippers in the MGM movie) carried her back to Kansas.

Dorothy was thirteen in 1906 when the great San Francisco earthquake dropped her and her cousin Zeb and his horse Jim into the earth's interior. The three, along with the Wizard who also was plummeted underground by the quake, were eventually rescued by Ozma, who teleported them to the Emerald City.

A few months after her return to Kansas—Ozma had used her Magic Belt to send Dorothy home—she and the hen Billina were on their way to Australia when a violent storm sank their ship. The pair were washed ashore in a chicken coop that floated them to Ev, an enchanted land west of Oz. Using a magic carpet to cross the Deadly Desert to Ev and back, Ozma rescued Dorothy and Billina from the wicked Nome King, along with Tik-Tok, a mechanical man Dorothy had found in Ev. Once again, Ozma's Magic Belt returned Dorothy to her aunt and uncle's farm in Kansas.

Dorothy was sixteen when she and Shaggy Man and Toto got lost on the roads near Butterfield. Johnny Doit's wooden sailboat, which he constructed in just a few minutes, carried the three across the Deadly Desert to Oz. Once more Dorothy was returned home by Ozma's Magic Belt.

In *The Emerald City of Oz*, Dorothy was teleported to Oz after going to the attic of her Kansas home and making a secret signal to Ozma. She was then seventeen. After granting Dorothy's wish to remain permanently in Oz, Ozma used her Magic Belt to bring Uncle Henry and Aunt Em to the Emerald City, where they could live forever with their niece.

Almost ninety years thus had passed before Dorothy made her trip to New York. She knew, of course, that all her childhood chums would no longer be living, including Cousin Zeb. He had been sent back to his home in California after his adventures underground with Dorothy and the Wizard. Dorothy remembered how cruelly Zeb had been treated by his parents and friends. None of them believed the wild tales he told about his adventures beneath the earth and his teleportation to Oz. Psychiatrists explained his long absence from home by saying he had wandered off somewhere suffering from amnesia, and was imagining all the strange events he claimed had really taken place.

Dorothy, too, had been dismayed by the refusal of her aunt and uncle to believe she had really been to Oz and Ev, and to lands below the earth's surface. Like Zeb, she had learned it was wise not to talk about those events because everyone always thought she was either lying or had lost her mind.

Such thoughts ran through Dorothy's head while she was taking a morning shower in Gold's apartment. She smiled when she recalled the astonishment on the faces of Uncle Henry and Aunt Em when they suddenly found themselves standing beside her in Ozma's palace.

Even though Dorothy knew that all her former friends were no longer alive, she was seized with an uncontrollable desire to see once more the region in Kansas where she had been so happy as a child.

"No problem," said Sammy Gold. "I'll have my secretary arrange for your round-trip by plane to Wichita, Kansas. From there you can take a bus to Butterfield. I'll reserve a room for you in Butterfield's best hotel. As I recall, your uncle's farm was close to Butterfield?"

"That's right. Our house was replaced by a new one after the tornado carried the old one to Oz. I wonder if the new house is still there. I'm told that Butterfield has grown so large that it may have swallowed Uncle Henry's farm. Anyway, I remember Butterfield so well that I'd love to see it again while I have the chance."

"You'll have your chance in a few days," said Gold. "As you agreed, I've hired a bodyguard for your companions. While you're away they'll be making a tour of radio and television shows around the country. Are you sure *you* don't need a bodyguard after what happened in Central Park?"

"I'm sure. I know I'll be all right." Dorothy was still reluctant to tell Mr. Gold about the pearls and her emerald ring.

The flight to Wichita was uneventful. When a bus dropped Dorothy off in Butterfield she was astounded by how much the village had changed. No longer was it the sleepy little town she remembered. Its only drugstore, where she once enjoyed ice-cream sodas with friends, was nowhere to be seen. Butterfield had become a bustling city with tall buildings and heavy traffic. She flagged a taxi and asked the driver to take her past the road which once had led to her uncle's farm.

The road was now a four-lane highway. When Dorothy reached the spot where the farmhouse once stood—the new one that had replaced the old house which blew away—she found it had become a region of high-rise apartments. There was not a single trace of anything she could recognize. The grade school she attended had long ago been torn down to make space for a supermarket. The little library where she had read with such delight the first five of Baum's Oz books had moved to another part of town and was ten times as large.

After returning to Wichita and boarding the plane that would take her back to New York, Dorothy slid her suitcase onto the rack above an aisle seat in the third row. When the plane became airborne, she was overcome with sadness about how thoroughly time can erase the sights and remove even the smells one recalls so fondly from childhood. But she was pleased to have made the trip.

"Butterfield may now be a big beautiful city," she said to herself, "but it's so crowded and noisy! I'm glad Ozma let me stay in Oz. And it was so good of her to bring my uncle and aunt there."

Dorothy was finally starting to feel homesick. Much as she liked Mr. Gold and was eager to help him, she was anxious to go home. She missed her uncle and aunt, Toto and Eureka, Betsy Bobbin and Trot, and Ozma, and all her other meat friends in Oz.

Dorothy's thoughts were suddenly interrupted by a loud shout of "Allah Akbar!" A swarthy-skinned young man, with a black mustache and goatee, had leaped to his feet at the rear of the plane and was walking rapidly down the aisle to the front. He turned to face the passengers. A large revolver was in his right hand.

"Please keep your seats," he said, "and don't get excited. I won't shoot anyone unless I have to. My name is Abdul. I'm taking over this plane."

A woman in a back seat began to scream.

"Shut up, lady!" Abdul shouted.

He waved his gun at one of the flight attendants. "You sit down, too. I see an empty seat over there."

Abdul turned his revolver toward another flight attendant who was also standing and looking very frightened. "Go see the pilots. Tell them to change course and head for Iraq."

Abdul raised both arms high in the air. "Long live Saddam Hussein!" he cried.

Everyone sat quiet and still, with looks of terror on their faces. Most of them were trembling.

"I have a bomb here," Abdul said as he tapped his free hand on a red box attached to the front of his belt. "If anyone tries to stop me, I'll press this button and blow us all to Paradise."

The woman who had screamed slumped down in her seat and fainted.

Dorothy was the only passenger who remained calm. She knew she had the blue and pink pearls in the toes of her shoes, and the white pearl was in the little green bag that hung on the gold cord around her neck.

While Abdul rattled on about the glories of Islam and the wickedness of Israel and the United States, Dorothy opened the green bag. She took out the white pearl and held it to her lips. "What can you tell me about this man," she whispered, "and what do you advise me to do?"

She moved the pearl close to her ear. "Abdul is bluffing," the pearl said in a voice so faint that only Dorothy could hear the words. "His bomb is a fake. His gun is not loaded. You can overcome him easily with the help of my blue sister. Assistance from my pink sister won't be necessary. Good luck!"

Dorothy replaced the white pearl in the bag, closed it, and shoved it back down inside her blouse. She stood up in the center of the aisle.

Abdul looked startled. "Sit down, madam," he said sternly as he pointed his revolver straight toward her. "Sit down unless you want to get yourself dead."

Dorothy did not reply and she did not sit down. Instead, she walked slowly forward. Abdul stepped back, more surprised than before. Behind him Dorothy saw one of the pilots emerge through the door to the cockpit, followed by the flight attendant who had just told him what was happening.

Dorothy reached out, snatched the gun from Abdul's hand, and tossed it over his head to the pilot. The pilot, looking as astonished as Abdul, caught the gun. Before he had a chance to grab the hijacker, Dorothy punched Abdul in the stomach.

He bent over with a loud *"Oof!"* Dorothy then raised a knee to bang the man under his chin. Abdul howled with pain.

An amazing thing now occurred. Dorothy seized Abdul's nose with her left hand. With her other hand between his legs, she lifted him high in the air, then tossed him backward over her head as if he were a sack of feathers. He landed with a thump, face down in the aisle behind her. Passengers clapped and cheered. The woman who had fainted opened her eyes and asked the man next to her what was going on.

"I can't imagine how you were able to do that," said the pilot, "but I sure thank you."

Dorothy stood aside while the pilot grabbed Abdul's feet and dragged him off to the cockpit. Abdul hid his face in his hands. He was blubbering like a baby.

"I can't do anything right!" he sobbed. "And such a young girl! I'm so humiliated! What will Mother think of me?"

The pilot phoned ahead to La Guardia Airport in New York. When the plane landed, three waiting FBI men handcuffed Abdul, pushed him into their limousine, and sped off. Dorothy was beseiged by a swarm of reporters and cameramen.

"We know you're Dorothy Gale who claims to be from Oz," one reporter said, "but we didn't know you knew karate. Are you a black belter? Did you learn to fight like that in Oz?"

"I don't know anything about karate," Dorothy replied. "I just did what I thought was the best thing to do."

"But how did you know the hijacker's gun wasn't loaded? How did you know his bomb was a fake?

Dorothy hesitated. "I just knew."

When Dorothy was back in her room in Gold's apartment, she took off her right shoe. The blue pearl that had given her superhuman strength had vanished. The silk bag that held the white pearl was also empty.

Dorothy removed her left shoe. The pink pearl was still there. How it knew it wouldn't be needed was hard to comprehend, but as I said before, Dorothy long ago stopped worrying about Oz magic.

Samuel Gold was at his studio in Hollywood when he heard on his office television set the news about the hijacking. He regretted that he hadn't given Dorothy a bodyguard in spite of her refusal, but apparently she didn't need one. What a girl!

Sammy smiled as he stroked Eureka. The cat had leaped into his lap and seemed to be sharing his thoughts. The publicity he was getting from the visit of Dorothy and her friends was truly priceless. It far exceeded anything he could have imagined.

19

19

BOGGS'S YACHT

W HEN BUFFALO Boggs heard what had happened in
Central Park he was so furious he could hardly speak.
He and the two brothers met once again for a conference in
the basement bar of a restaurant in Little Italy.

"Any idiot knows a knife can't fly through the air like a
bird," Buffalo roared at Mugsy, "and jab your backside and
slice your belt. I don't believe a word you say. Are you trying
to tell me Dorothy is some kind of witch? She's no witch.
She's just a good-looking young actress Gold has hired to pretend she's from Oz."

Boggs pounded his fist on the table. "This is the second
time you and your stupid brother have bungled everything.

Forget about my offer. You're both fired. Go away! Go bump off somebody else!"

"Don't talk to us like that," said Bugsy, "or you might get your legs broke."

Buffalo snorted like a buffalo. "I don't scare easy. You two bums couldn't harm Uncle Wiggily. Now beat it! Scram! I'll take care of Dorothy and those two phonies myself."

The brothers didn't budge. "Please, Mr. Boggs," whined Bugsy, "you know I don't mean what I said. We ain't goin' to harm you after all you done for us. We need the dough. Please, boss, give us another chance."

Boggs slowly placed on an ashtray the foul-smelling cigar he had been puffing. After glancing back and forth from one twin to the other he finally said: "Okay. I'll let you bums try one more time. We have to get rid of the girl and her two wacko pals. Now listen carefully. Here's my plan."

Boggs's evil plan was as follows. He owned a huge diesel-driven yacht that he kept anchored in the harbor at the southern tip of Manhattan Island where the Hudson River empties into the Atlantic. Samuel Gold also owned a yacht that he kept tied up in the same harbor.

"You can be sure Dorothy knows all about Gold's yacht," Boggs said, keeping his voice low. "I'll have my secretary phone her as soon as Gold is back in Hollywood. She'll pretend she's one of Gold's assistants. I'll instruct her to say that Sammy wants to send her and her friends on a vacation cruise to the Bahamas. It will be a reward for the great job they've been doing. She'll explain that Gold regrets he can't join them, but that his ship's captain will take good care of them. I'll send a limousine to pick them up and take them to the harbor."

"Brilliant!" exclaimed Mugsy with a twisted grin. "You always know better than us how to handle such things."

"That's because I'm smart and you two are nitwits. I'll join you later on board my yacht."

"How do you want us to do the job?" Bugsy asked.

"We'll wait until it's dark and the ship is far out to sea. You can then toss each of them overboard. That tin contraption will sink to the bottom of the ocean. Even if Dorothy and whoever is inside that Scarecrow outfit can swim, the shore will be too far away for them to reach it."

"Won't your crew wonder what happened to the passengers?" asked Bugsy.

"Yes, but they all have prison records and they're all indebted to me. I'll pay them well to back up the story that the ship was hit by a fierce storm, then a big wave swept over the deck and washed Dorothy and her friends over the side."

Boggs chuckled with glee as he thought about his wicked scheme. He rubbed his palms together. They were so grimy that the rubbing made tiny balls of dirt that showered down into and around his glass of beer.

Dorothy suspected nothing when she got the phone call from Boggs's secretary. She knew Mr. Gold was in Hollywood to begin hiring script writers and computer artists to work on his production of *The Emerald City of Oz*. Dorothy said on the phone that she understood why Gold would be unable to join them.

Although Dorothy had once traveled on a ship bound for Australia, she had never been to the Bahamas. What a splendid way, she thought, to end her visit to Earth. And how generous of Mr. Gold to arrange it! She was sure that her companions would also greatly enjoy a sea voyage.

Buffalo gave careful instructions to his crew. They were told to pretend that the yacht belonged to Samuel Gold. They were told to treat the Scarecrow and the Tin Woodman as if they were ordinary people. The straw man, Boggs explained, was a skilled actor dressed in a costume that included a cloth mask over his face. The tin man was some sort of robot. No one understood how he worked. Mugsy and Bugsy were instructed to remain in their cabins until nightfall. When the time was right they would emerge and heave Dorothy and her pals over the edge of the deck.

Boggs's limousine drove the three unsuspecting passengers to the harbor. As they walked up the gangplank of Buffalo's yacht, he was on hand to greet them as the ship's captain. He was certain none of the three had seen him before. However, to make sure they wouldn't recognize him from photographs, he had put on a fake red beard, dyed his mustache red, and covered his bald head with a red wig.

"Welcome aboard, my friends," Boggs said. "I'm Captain Horatio Blowhorn. Mr. Gold sends his deep regrets that he couldn't join us. Seaman Smith here will take your suitcase and show you to your cabins."

After the yacht had sailed many miles from land, Dorothy and her friends enjoyed a stroll around the deck. She took deep breaths of the fresh ocean breezes. The sea was so calm that there was not the slightest rocking of the yacht. Dorothy was grateful for such smooth sailing because on the first day of her voyage to Australia she had been dreadfully seasick.

Seagulls were following the yacht. They made little squealing sounds as they watched for garbage to be dumped into the water, then they would swoop down for a feast. Dorothy was startled when a flying fish leaped out of the ocean and landed on the deck near her feet. A sailor picked it up and let her examine it before he tossed it back into the sea.

That evening, after the sun had set and the dark sky glittered with a million stars, the Tin Woodman leaned his axe against the deck's railing and peered down. He was fascinated by the eerie luminescence of the waves as they churned past the yacht's side to form a trail of light in the ship's wake. High overhead a new moon looked like a thin white fingernail.

Mugsy and Bugsy had been secretly following the tin man, and were waiting like crouching cats for the time when he would be alone. The time was now. They tiptoed up behind him, one on each side, and lifted him easily. They flung him over the railing.

Being hollow, the Tin Woodman floated for a while on the ocean's surface while the ship chugged on. Boggs was right in guessing he would soon sink. His body was far from airtight. Water began to seep through the cracks around the little door on his chest. When his body was completely filled with salt water, it stopped his silk heart from beating. Slowly the tin man began to sink.

The woodman waved his arms in circles like the arms of a windmill as he tried to swim upward, but it was no use. He was several yards below the surface when a giant shark approached and tried to bite him. When her teeth failed to penetrate the hard metal, the shark decided that the thing she bit, whatever it was, was not fit to eat. She glided away to look elsewhere for a meal.

As the helpless tin man was nearing the ocean's floor a dolphin came swimming by. "Great Neptune!" he shouted. "It's the Tin Woodman!"

"I am indeed he," said the tin man. "But who are you? How did you recognize me? And how is it you speak excellent English?"

"It's a long sad story," said the dolphin, "but before I tell it, let's get you on my back so I can carry you up to the surface. It will be easier there for us to talk and hear each other. You can tell me how you, of all people, managed to get yourself in such a terrible fix."

The dolphin dived under the tin man, between his legs, then rose until the woodman was comfortably astride his rescuer. When the dolphin reached the surface, the Tin Woodman opened the door on his chest to let the seawater pour out.

"It's a good thing I'm nickel-plated," he said, "or this icy salt water would surely have damaged my tin." It was not long until his silk heart had dried out enough to start beating again.

For several hours, while the dolphin carried his passenger through the night toward New York, the pair conversed.

"I once lived in the Nonestic Ocean," said the dolphin. "As you know, all animals in Oz and close to Oz, even those in the sea, can talk. One day, when I happened to be exploring the Atlantic, Glinda suddenly moved Oz to another universe. No one had warned me she would do that. It left me stranded here."

"But how is it you still can talk? I always thought animals talk only when they are in or close to Oz."

"I suppose this doesn't apply to sea life—only to animals on land. Anyhow, I can still think and speak as good as I always could."

The Tin Woodman explained how he and the Scarecrow and Dorothy had been invited to New York by a Hollywood movie producer named Samuel Gold to help promote a motion picture he planned to make about Oz. He told the dolphin how an evil rival of Gold's had been trying to kill all three of them.

"I don't know who threw me into the sea. It was dark and I never saw their faces. My guess is they were the same men who tried to murder me and Scarecrow when we were on top of a tall building. One of them later tried to kill Dorothy."

The dolphin swerved a bit to avoid hitting an octopus who was floating on the sea. "I can understand how it would be hard to kill you or your straw friend, but Dorothy is flesh and blood like me. If she's still on that yacht she must be in grave danger."

"Not in as much danger as you might think. Ozma's keeping a close watch over her with her Magic Picture. And Dorothy has a pink pearl in her shoe that will protect her."

"You mean one of the three enchanted pearls from the Island of Pingaree?"

"The very ones. Inga gave them to Ozma on one of her birthdays, and Ozma let Dorothy borrow them for her trip to New York. She's already used the blue pearl and the white one. But how did you know about those pearls? I'm amazed by how much you know about Oz."

"You forget," said the dolphin, "that a river runs near the Emerald City. It starts high in the northern mountains of the Gillikin country, flows across Oz past the Emerald City, then turns west to flow under the Deadly Desert to Ev. From Ev it empties into the Nonestic Ocean. I often swam up this river to the Emerald City, where I could chat with anyone who came to the river's bank. I became good friends with Dorothy and Ozma, and with the Cowardly Lion, Toto, and lots of other important persons who live in the city."

The Tin Woodman brought the dolphin up to date on most of the major events that happened in Oz since Glinda moved Oz off the earth. The dolphin in turn recounted some of his adventures in the Atlantic after he became trapped there. On one occasion, during the Second World War, he had surfaced and said "Good afternoon" to an officer on the deck of a destroyer escort. The officer was so terrified that the dolphin decided it was best not to say anything to humans outside of Oz.

"Of course the other dolphins in the Atlantic can't talk as I can, but we dolphins have a language of our own that I never forgot how to speak and understand. It's based on high-frequency whistles. I've made lots of dolphin friends in the Atlantic."

"May I ask your name?"

"It's Zoroaster. My mother named me after the Wizard's second name. Friends all call me Zo. I like the nickname because it's Oz spelled backward."

"I used to be called Nick Chopper, but nobody calls me that since I lost my meat body."

"I know your history," said Zo. "Dorothy once told me all about it."

When the dolphin reached New York harbor it was almost midnight. He swam slowly up the East River to let the tin man step ashore at a spot not far from Gold's apartment.

"I can't thank you enough, Zo," said the Tin Woodman. "If you hadn't noticed me I would still be at the bottom of the sea. I hope there's something I can do for you someday to repay your kindness."

"There is. I long desperately to return to my homeland, or rather my home sea—the Nonestic Ocean. I have a good wife there and many children and hundreds of grandchildren. Maybe you could ask Glinda if there's some way I can get back home."

"There well may be. Ozma's Magic Belt no longer can teleport living creatures or nonliving objects back and forth between the two universes. But, as you surely know, Glinda's knowledge of sorcery is awesome. I'll speak to her about your request as soon as I can."

"Thank you, thank you," said Zoroaster. "I hope you and Dorothy and Scarecrow make it back to Oz safely. I couldn't understand a word you said about that thing you called a Klein Bottle. Even if I could force my way up through it with my flippers, there's no way I can get from the Atlantic to that park in New York where you say the bottle hangs in the air."

"Don't lose hope," said the tin man. "I'm sure Glinda will figure out a way to bring you home."

"It was a great honor to have helped you," said Zo. "I know from what Ozma told me how kind you are to all the animals in Oz, even to little insects. And I've heard how justly you rule over the Winkies."

The Tin Woodman thanked Zoroaster once more as he patted him on the nose and said good-bye. The dolphin raised himself high enough above the water to wave a front flipper. Then he turned and swam rapidly down the East River.

The Tin Woodman did his best to shake the water off his feet and legs before he began to walk westward through the night, across Manhattan, on his way to Fifth Avenue.

20

MORE NARROW ESCAPES

AFTER DISPOSING of the tin man, Mugsy and Bugsy, still on Boggs's yacht, turned their attention to Dorothy. She had retired to her cabin and was about to undress and put on pajamas when the brothers burst into her room. Standing behind her, Mugsy pressed a hand over her mouth to keep her from screaming. With his other arm he circled her waist. Mugsy grabbed her legs. They carried her to the ship's railing.

The ship had encountered a dense fog that was moving westward—a fog so thick that the ocean's surface couldn't be seen when one looked down. Dorothy, having given up struggling to get free, decided that screaming would be of no help.

She wondered what the pink pearl would do. The brothers swung her back and forth several times, like a hammock, then heaved her over the railing.

A split second before Dorothy struck the dark water, she rose slowly in the air and floated back over the railing to land on her feet next to the astonished twins. Before they had time to think about what had happened, they felt themselves lifted upward.

Each of the brothers turned several somersaults in the air before they remained suspended several yards above the deck. They glared down at Dorothy, fear and amazement on their faces.

Dorothy glanced up and shook her fist at the twins. Something inside her brain, perhaps coming from the pink pearl, prompted her to say, "It's time you boys had a bath."

Over the railing they went. Dorothy could hear the splashes when they dropped headfirst into the sea.

Boggs had been watching all this through a window of the pilot's room, where his first mate was at the wheel steering the yacht. Even though the deck was well lit, it was not easy to see through the swirling mist. As far as Buffalo could make out, it looked as if Dorothy had mysteriously returned to the deck after being tossed overboard. And now his two assassins seemed to have leaped over the ship's railing into the sea.

"Stop the engine!" Boggs shouted to his first mate. "Men overboard!"

Buffalo grabbed two life preservers from a shelf on the bulkhead, then rushed out of the pilot's room to the ship's railing. He flung the preservers over the edge, then turned to scowl fiercely at Dorothy.

"I don't know what's going on here, Miss Gale, but you

should know that your robot buddy is now at the bottom of the Atlantic. It's your turn to join him!"

Buffalo took a pistol from a holster strapped under his jacket. He aimed it at Dorothy's heart and was about to pull the trigger when the pink pearl acted again. The gun was wrenched from his hand. In midair it turned slowly around then fired several shots that struck the deck a few inches from Buffalo's shoes.

Dorothy was surprised by the fact that the pistol made no noise when it fired. Later, when she thought about it, she realized that the pink pearl was making sure the sounds of gunfire would not alert the pilot or the seamen who were below the main deck.

Buffalo leaped backward. Looking up, his eyes wide open with terror, he saw the gun rise high above the deck. For a few seconds it remained fixed in space, still aimed at Boggs, then it turned around to plunge through the fog and over the railing. Dorothy thought she heard the splash when it hit the water.

Boggs had completely forgotten he was not wearing his wig and false whiskers. "Well I declare!" exclaimed Dorothy, "if it isn't Buffalo Boggs! I recognize you from a magazine picture Mr. Gold showed me. You must be one of the most evil men in America. I'm beginning to understand now how you tricked us. This isn't Mr. Gold's yacht. It's yours!"

Dorothy noticed that the Tin Woodman's axe was leaning against the ship's railing where he had left it. She picked it up, raised it high in the air, and walked slowly toward Buffalo.

Trembling with fright and about to cry, Boggs got down on his knees and clasped his hands. "Please, Dorothy, please!"

he blubbered. "Don't hurt me! Have pity on an old man. I swear I'll never try to harm you or your friends again. You want a million dollars? I'll give you a million dollars. Just don't touch me with that axe."

"I have no intention of harming you," said Dorothy, "as long as you behave and do what I say. I don't want any money. We never use money in Oz. Besides, I don't trust you. You'll say anything to save your skin. Now take me to the Scarecrow before I change my mind and chop off that miserable head of yours."

"Yes, yes, of course! I'll do whatever you say." Boggs was shaking so hard that Dorothy could hear his false teeth rattle.

They found the Scarecrow sitting in his room, reading a copy of *Time* magazine he had found on a table. There was a picture of him on the cover, standing beside Dorothy and the Tin Woodman.

"Hello, Dorothy," said the straw man. "Why are you carrying my friend's axe? And who is this frightened chap with the chattering teeth?"

"He's Buffalo Boggs. We're not on Mr. Gold's yacht. The ship belongs to Boggs."

"You're telling me this is Buffalo Odersby Boggs, Mr. Gold's sworn enemy? Does he always smell this bad?"

"I wouldn't be surprised," replied Dorothy. "He just tried to shoot me but the pink pearl snatched away his gun. Remember those two men who threw you off the Empire State Building and tried to kill the Tin Woodman?"

"How could I forget!"

"Well, they've been hiding on this yacht. They work for Mr. Boggs. The pink pearl just tossed them into the sea, but not before they had done the same thing with our tin friend."

The Scarecrow leaped to his feet and slapped Buffalo as hard as he could. Of course his cloth hand, stuffed with straw, had little effect. "Let's throw *him* overboard!"

"We can't do that," said Dorothy, "even though he deserves it."

"In that case," said the straw man, "I suggest you press your ring."

Dorothy pressed it. The three watched it turn crimson.

Ozma was having breakfast in the dining room of her palace when her emerald ring glowed red and began to chime. She grabbed her ebony wand from a side table, then rushed to the room where the Magic Picture hung on a wall beside her Magic Belt. She drew the curtains that covered the picture. "Show me Dorothy," she commanded.

To give Ozma time to get to the Magic Picture, Dorothy turned to face Boggs. He was still too terrified to speak. "You never believed that my friends and I are really from Oz. Have you changed your mind now that you saw what happened to your two thugs? Was it too foggy to see me float back to the deck after they tossed me over the railing? Was it too foggy to see your two men sail over the railing, turn upside down, and drop headfirst into the ocean? And how do you account for what happened to your pistol?"

Boggs remained silent. "I must be hallucinating," he thought. "These things can't be happening." He stared at Dorothy's hand when he heard her ring start to chime.

Dorothy raised the axe she was still holding and shook its blade in Boggs's face. "Now watch closely," she said, sounding like a stage magician about to vanish an elephant. "You're going to see something that will boggle your mind—something you'll never ever understand."

Dorothy raised her free hand to make a secret sign. It told Ozma, "We're in danger. Get us out of here!"

When Ozma saw that Dorothy was holding the tin man's axe, she guessed at once that something terrible must have happened to him. She had no idea who the bald man was, although she knew they were on a ship at sea. In a flash she decided that the best thing to do was to teleport Dorothy and the Scarecrow back to Gold's apartment in Manhattan.

Princess Ozma raised her slender black wand and moved its silver tip in a large spiral, seven times clockwise, then thirteen times the other way. At the same time she spoke some sentences in a strange tongue that only the good witches of Oz understand.

Buffalo's jaw dropped and he almost passed out. Before his very eyes Dorothy and the Scarecrow completely disappeared!

Ozma next asked the picture to show her the Tin Woodman. She was surprised to see him sitting calmly on the back of a large black-and-white dolphin. They seemed to be conversing while the dolphin swam through a dense fog.

"Why, I believe that's Zoroaster!" Ozma exclaimed. "I've often wondered what became of him after Oz moved to another universe."

Because the tin man seemed in no danger, Ozma decided not to intervene. Teleporting, she knew, could be dangerous. Accidents can occur that often are hard to rectify. Like Glinda and other good witches of Oz, it was Ozma's practice never to teleport living creatures unless it seemed absolutely necessary.

It was past midnight in Manhattan and the sidewalks were almost deserted when the Tin Woodman began his crosstown walk toward Gold's apartment. A few passersby stared at him through the fog. A tall man with a long gray beard handed him a card on which was printed a biblical verse from Matthew 24. Beneath the verse a paragraph warned that next month New York City would be destroyed by fire from heaven unless its citizens repented of their sins.

Near the middle of a poorly lit street stood a girl—she seemed no older than fifteen—who was wearing tight-fitting shorts and high-heeled boots. She thought the man approaching might be a good customer until she recognized him as the famous Tin Woodman she had seen on television. She wisely decided not to invite him to her hotel room, but she stopped him anyway.

"May I have your autograph?" she asked. From her jacket she took a ballpoint pen.

"Certainly, madam," said the tin man. "Do you have a piece of paper?"

The girl shook her head.

The Tin Woodman remembered the card he was holding. He took the pen from the girl, turned over the card, then held the pen a few inches above the card's blank back. "And your name?"

"Just write Annabelle." She spelled the name.

The tin man wrote on the card: FOR ANNABELLE, FROM THE TIN WOODMAN OF OZ, EMPEROR OF THE WINKIES.

Annabelle smiled when she read what the tin man had written. She put the pen and card in her pocket. "Thank you very much, sir."

"My pleasure," said the woodman. He tipped his funnel hat before he strode off through the gloom.

Thirty minues later, when he entered Gold's apartment, he was astonished to find Dorothy and the Scarecrow sitting in the living room. They jumped to their feet to greet him warmly, as surprised to see him as he was to see them. The Scarecrow embraced his old friend. Dorothy kissed him on the cheek.

"Am I right in guessing you used the ring?" the Tin Woodman asked Dorothy.

"Yes. Ozma saw we were in danger, and when I made our secret sign she brought us both here. Now tell us—how in the world did you manage to escape from the Atlantic and make it here?"

"It's hard to believe, Dorothy, but I was rescued by a friendly dolphin who once lived in the Nonestic Ocean. He said he knew you and Ozma. His name is Zoroaster."

"Zoroaster!" Dorothy shouted. "That's incredible! Yes, Zo's an old friend. He liked to take me riding on his back in the Emerald River. Then he stopped visiting the city. We haven't seen him since Glinda moved Oz and its surroundings off the earth. Why is he living in the North Atlantic?"

"I'll tell you all about him later," said the tin man. "He saved me from a fate worse than death. I see you brought along my axe. I missed it terribly when I was riding on Zo. I always feel naked without it."

Dorothy picked up the axe from where she had leaned it against the brick side of the fireplace, and handed it to her friend. "It's lucky I happened to be holding it when Ozma brought me here."

The three old pals stayed up for hours, talking about recent events and trying to figure out the best way to thwart Buffalo's evil schemes. They all agreed that he and his two hired killers deserved some sort of punishment. Should they go to the police and try to have Boggs arrested? Would the police believe he had tried to murder them? Gold had told Dorothy about some of Boggs's earlier crimes, and how his high-priced attorneys always managed to keep him out of prison.

It was almost dawn when Dorothy finally went to bed. As she had expected, the pink pearl was no longer in her shoe. With a sinking feeling in her stomach, she realized that without the pink pearl's protection she could be in even greater danger than before.

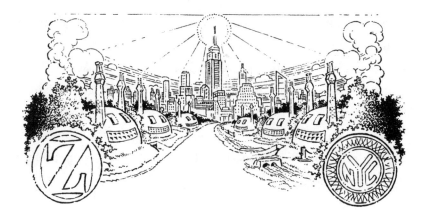

21

≈≈≈

THE WATER OF OBLIVION

Y OU WILL recall that after Boggs stopped his yacht he tossed two life preservers into the sea. Mugsy and Bugsy swam toward them, barely able to see them through the thick fog. Each grabbed a preserver. Cursing and spitting out salt water, they paddled their way toward the motionless ship's port side.

On deck, still shaken and dumbfounded by seeing Dorothy and the Scarecrow vanish, Boggs ordered one of his sailors to lower a rope ladder over the ship's side. The twins, dripping wet and still shouting curses, climbed aboard.

At Boggs's command, his pilot turned the yacht around to head back to New York. What he and his hired felons talked about on the trip back is anybody's guess. I suspect that all three were now convinced they were the victims of some mysterious and powerful sorcery, or perhaps they feared they were going mad.

Dorothy phoned Samuel Gold to tell him what had happened on Buffalo's yacht, and how he had tricked them into coming aboard. Gold was so disturbed by this news that he flew at once to New York in his private jet to discuss the situation with Dorothy and her companions. The four met in the living room of Gold's apartment.

"We now know for certain that Mugsy and Bugsy work for Boggs," Gold said to Dorothy. "But could we prove in a court of law that they tried to kill you? Boggs is a wealthy man. He can hire the best lawyers. So far they've always managed to keep him out of jail. There must be *some* way we can put an end to his evil schemes."

"I could chop off his head," said the Tin Woodman as he raised and shook his axe. "But that wouldn't be kind. My heart would never allow it."

"Not to mention," added Gold. "that you would surely be arrested and maybe sent to the electric chair."

"I doubt if my old friend could be electrocuted," said the Scarecrow, "although the current might stop his heart from beating. You can't electrocute tin. With me it's different. The current could set my straw on fire and burn me to ashes."

Gold spread his chubby hands in a gesture of hopelessness. "So—what can we do?"

"I can't think of anything," said the tin man. "My brain is not of the highest quality. But Scarecrow should be able to come up with something."

The straw man had been scratching his head with a middle finger, and thinking as hard as he could.

Suddenly he jumped to his feet. "Eureka! I've got it!"

"You've got what?" Dorothy asked.

"The Forbidden Fountain!"

"Of course!" Dorothy exclaimed. "Why didn't *I* think of that?"

"Because," said the Scarecrow, "pretty as you are, my dear, you don't have my superior brains."

Gold also understood at once. As an Oz fan since childhood, when his mother first read to him *The Wizard of Oz*, he knew all about the Forbidden Fountain and its enchanted water. It played a key role in the plot of the movie he was planning. He recalled how the evil Nome King led his army of Whimsies, Growleywogs, and Phanfasms through an underground tunnel with plans to emerge outside Ozma's palace and seize control of her throne. It had been the Scarecrow who thought of using Ozma's Magic Belt to fill the tunnel with dust so that when the invaders came out of the tunnel, near the Forbidden Fountain, they would be extremely thirsty. The plan worked beautifully. When the soldiers drank the Water of Oblivion they instantly forgot who they were and why they were there.

Unfortunately, the Nome King later recovered his memory and became as wicked as before. As was revealed in *The Magic of Oz*, the Nome had to be given a second dose of the enchanted liquid.

"Our problem now," said Gold, "is how to get a sample of the Water of Oblivion from Oz to here."

"Are you sure it will work outside Oz?" Dorothy asked.

"Good question," said Sammy. "I'll try to reach Glinda this

afternoon and ask. Of course she'll know. She knows everything."

Glinda replied at once to Gold's E-mail letter. Yes, she
typed on her computer, the liquid would work anywhere on
Earth. After all, she reminded Gold, it provided water for the
River Lethe that flowed through the Hades of the ancient
Greeks. She promised to get in touch with Ozma to discuss
ways of sending some of the forbidden water to New York.

After a long phone conversation with Glinda, Ozma consulted her old friend the Wizard. As all Oz fans know, he had
been thoroughly trained by Glinda in the arts of Oz magic.
No longer was he the humbug who had floated to Oz more
than a century ago in a circus balloon.

"It's not possible to teleport the water to Earth," the Wizard
informed Ozma. "Even if we could, I suspect the teleporting
process would destroy the water's power to erase memory. In
my opinion, and I think Glinda would agree, the only way to
deliver the water is to drop it through the Klein Bottle. I
suggest you have someone fill a plastic bottle with some of
the liquid. Glinda can send one of her winged monkeys to
carry the container to Ballville and there drop it into the
bottle. We'll have to decide, of course, on the precise time for
the drop, then let Mr. Gold know the hour so he can be sure
someone is in Central Park to catch the container."

The time for the drop was set for four in the morning, New
York time, on the following Thursday. Dorothy was still half
asleep that morning when she and her friends entered the
park and walked to the spot where the Klein Bottle was suspended in the air. The invisible portion of its tube was about
fifteen feet above a grassy knoll near the reservoir.

As the time approached four, the Scarecrow positioned himself below the spot where he judged the Klein Bottle was hanging, his padded arms outstretched to catch the container. "Is it time yet?" he asked.

Dorothy consulted her wristwatch. "It's exactly four."

Down from the inky black sky, from the hands of a winged monkey, came the container. It missed the straw man's arms by several feet, but being plastic it bounced on the soft turf without breaking. The Scarecrow picked it up carefully and handed it to the Tin Woodman. Luckily, no visitors to the park were around to see what happened, except for a brown squirrel that flicked its tail and appeared puzzled.

The Tin Woodman opened his chest and put the container of water inside.

As the three walked back to Gold's apartment on Fifth Avenue, a breeze blew against their faces with such force that they could hardly hear what they each were saying.

"It sure is windy," said the Scarecrow.

"Not so," replied the tin man. "Today is Thursday."

"How could you be thirsty? You know we don't drink."

"Cut the comedy," said Dorothy. "The next thing you two clowns will be doing is 'Who's on first?' "

"I thought Who was on second," said the Scarecrow.

Dorothy punched his shoulder so hard it almost knocked him over.

"Sorry about that, Dorothy," said the straw man. "Every now and then, at Oz benefit performances, Nick and I entertain the crowd with old comedy routines. We learned them from one of the Wizard's stand-up comedy pills."

The Scarecrow spent what was left of the night trying to think of ways to get the Water of Oblivion to Mr. Boggs and his two hit men. While Dorothy was having breakfast, he outlined the following plan.

"First we must take care of Mugsy and Bugsy. We know about the bar in Little Italy where they like to hang out. Nick and I will disguise ourselves as men who work for Mr. Gold. We'll approach the twins with an offer of, say, a hundred thousand dollars to bump off their boss. I doubt if they'll refuse that much money. As soon as we get a chance, we'll pour some of the magic water into their beer."

Dorothy took a sip of coffee, then shook her head. "There's no way that could work. The brothers will know who you are. How can you and Nick make yourselves look like ordinary meat people?"

"Easy," said the tin man. "We'll wear business suits."

"But," Dorothy protested, "your faces will give you away."

"Rubber masks," said the Scarecrow.

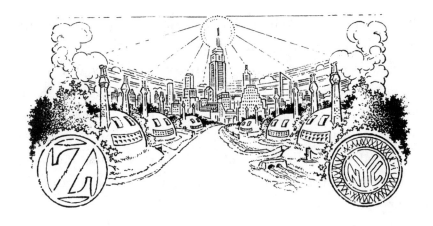

22

<hr/>

THE FATE
OF THE TWINS

Samuel Gold was enthusiastic about the Scarecrow's plan. He purchased suits and shoes of correct sizes for the two friends. Experts in his props department prepared two extremely lifelike masks of middle-aged white men. Using a screwdriver they removed the tin man's long nose. Wigs were added. The woodman's funnel was replaced by a black felt hat. The Scarecrow was given a similar hat. The two men put on white shirts, pinstriped suits, bow ties, black socks, black gloves, and black shoes. Over their masks they wore dark green sunglasses.

After the studio's makeup department put finishing touches on the rubber masks, their transformation into men of flesh and blood was so convincing that when Dorothy first saw them she didn't believe Mr. Gold when he told her who they were.

Sammy hired a private detective to keep watch on the bar in Little Italy. When he saw the brothers go inside, he telephoned Gold from his car. Gold's private limousine then took the disguised Scarecrow and Tin Woodman to the bar. Gold had carefully rehearsed them on how to behave and what to say.

Mugsy and Bugsy were sitting opposite each other at a booth in the rear of the bar. They were munching pretzels and guzzling beer. The Scarecrow and the tin man walked over to the booth without removing their hats or dark glasses. The straw man carried an empty briefcase.

"My name is James Blue," said the Scarecrow. "This is my associate Thomas Green. We were sent here by Samuel Gold. He wants to offer you a hundred thousand dollars to do a job for him."

Mugsy put his glass slowly down on the table and moved closer to the wall. "Have a seat. For that much dough we're interested. Tell us more."

Blue and Green took seats beside the twins.

"We are aware," said the tin man, "that Mr. Boggs hired you to destroy Dorothy and those two clowns who claim to be from Oz. As you must realize now, they're not so easy to destroy. We don't know why. They seem to be protected by some kind of supernatural forces. We've been told that Mr. Boggs has withdrawn his offer."

"You got it right," said Bugsy. "The boss told us the deal was kaput."

"In that case," the Scarecrow continued, "Mr. Gold has a

much better offer. It should be easy to carry out. I have here in this briefcase . . ." He paused to lift up the briefcase and pat it with his gloved hand. "We have here fifty thousand dollars in unmarked bills. Mr. Gold wants you to get rid of Boggs. You can do it any way you like. If you agree, the cash here is yours. You get the rest when Buffalo is dead."

The twins squinted at each other with raised eyebrows. "Give us a few minutes," said Mugsy, "to talk it over."

Blue and Green stood up alongside the booth so the brothers could leave and go to the men's room. As soon as they were out of sight, the Scarecrow took a small bottle from a side pocket of his jacket. He poured half of its contents into Mugsy's beer and emptied the other half into the glass where Bugsy had been sitting.

The twins were smiling crookedly and squinting with one eye when they returned to the booth.

"We'll be delighted to do the job," said Mugsy. "Boggs paid us okay, but he always treated us like dirt. To tell you the truth, we hated his guts. We'll be glad to get rid of him."

Mugsy called to the waitress. "Two beers for our friends."

After the waitress brought the beer, the four men raised their glasses and clinked them together. "Good-bye Mr. Boggs," said Bugsy. The brothers drained their glasses. Blue and Green put their filled glasses back on the table without even pretending to take a swallow.

"How do you plan to kill Boggs?" the tin man asked.

There was a long period of silence. "Boggs? Boggs?" said Mugsy. "Who's Boggs?"

"And who are you?" asked Bugsy. "Do we know you?"

Blue and Green got up from the booth. The Scarecrow

picked up the empty briefcase. "Don't forget to pay the waitress," he said.

"Why are you leaving?" asked Mugsy. "Come to think of it, why are we here? And where is here? And who are we, anyway?"

Bugsy was looking just as bewildered. He turned to face his twin brother. "Who are you? How come you look exactly like me?"

Later that afternoon the twins were picked up by two policemen in a squad car. The brothers had been wandering around Little Italy, muttering to themselves and acting strangely. They were taken to Bellevue Hospital for observation.

That night, in Gold's apartment while watching the evening news on television, Dorothy and her friends learned that the brothers had been arrested and identified by their fingerprints. They were said to be two ex-convicts who were out of prison on parole. Psychiatrists at Bellevue were treating them for extreme amnesia.

Samuel Gold, at his home in California, also heard the news. He telephoned Dorothy to congratulate the Scarecrow and Tin Woodman. "Tell them how pleased I am with how well they did the job. Wonderful! That should take care of those two scoundrels for quite a while. Do you know how long the oblivion lasts?"

"According to the Wizard," Dorothy answered, "it lasts at least several years. Most persons who drink the water *never* get back their memory. They have to start life all over again like little children."

"Let's hope that's the case," said Gold. "Now we must think of the best way to get Buffalo to taste the magic water."

The twins were released from Bellevue several months later, when they were finally well enough to take care of themselves. The last I heard, Mugsy was working for a septic tank company in Yonkers, New York. Bugsy had a job collecting garbage in Secaucus, New Jersey.

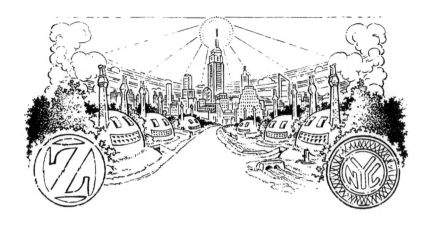

23

A TRAP IS SET

AFTER THE Water of Oblivion had done its work on Mugsy and Bugsy, Samuel Gold flew Dorothy and her friends to Hollywood in his private plane. Only a small portion of the magic water had been used, and the Tin Woodman still carried the rest of it inside his chest. Now it was Boggs's turn to drink some of the enchanted liquid.

The Scarecrow suggested the following scenario. Gold would invite Buffalo to his studio for lunch, presumably to discuss plans for their blockbuster musicals. Sammy was not sure Boggs would accept. If he did, they would serve him a meal that included a large portion of salted herring. The herring would make him very thirsty.

Because Sammy never drank anything containing alcohol, his studio's dining hall, unlike most studio dining rooms in Hollywood, never served alcoholic beverages—not even wine or beer. It did, however, provide guests with tall glasses of ice water.

Gold instructed a waitress to see that Boggs's glass of water would contain several spoonfuls of the Water of Oblivion.

Sammy was surprised when Boggs accepted his invitation. As Buffalo entered a small private dining room adjacent to the main room, his beady eyes kept shifting from side to side as if he expected some sort of trap. He had been seeing a psychiatrist who convinced him that the events he thought to have taken place on his yacht were delusions caused by a drug overdose. He glanced nervously at Dorothy and her two companions before he took a seat between Gold and the tin man.

Sammy opened the conversation by saying, "I understand, Buffalo, that your friends Mugsy and Bugsy are in a mental hospital suffering from amnesia. Is that true?"

"They're not *my* friends," Boggs lied. "I never heard of them until I read about them in the *Los Angeles Times*."

Gold pointed to Dorothy. "Are you convinced now that this young woman is really Dorothy Gale from Kansas?"

Boggs snorted so loudly that it blew a pink carnation out of a vase at the center of the table. "Do you think I'm a fool, Sam? Everybody knows you pretend she's from Oz just to get publicity for your musical. Everybody knows that this creep opposite me is an actor dressed and made up to look like a scarecrow. Everybody knows that this metal machine sitting here is a fiendishly ingenious robot. I have no idea how the damn thing works, but I do know somebody's controlling his speech and body movements."

"If that's true," said Sammy, "how can you explain the fact that the Tin Woodman has appeared on dozens of talk shows around the country? No one has ever seen anyone nearby who could be operating him."

Boggs shook his head. "As I said, I don't know how he's animated, but I'm not such an idiot as to think a man made entirely of tin could be alive, or that Oz is anything but an imaginary land invented by L. Frank Baum."

"What about me?" Dorothy asked. "Am I also a phony?"

"You're an extremely beautiful young woman," said Boggs, "and a very clever actress. I assume Sam expects you to star in his film. Otherwise, why would he go to all the trouble and expense of hiring you to pretend you're Dorothy Gale? I don't know who you are, but you can't be what you say you are. Dorothy Gale and her uncle and aunt disappeared from their farm near Butterfield more than eighty years ago. They haven't been seen since. No one knows what happened to them. Of course they would all be dead by now. If Dorothy were alive somewhere she'd be older than a hundred. You can't be more than twenty."

Dorothy smiled and said nothing.

"How are things going with your Peter Pan plans?" Gold asked while the waitress served them plates of herring and glasses of water.

Boggs rubbed a hand over his bald head and grinned. "Great! Madonna has agreed to play Peter. We already are teaching her how to use those invisible wires that make it look like she's flying. I've hired Roseanne to play Tinkerbell. Of course we'll use computer techniques to make her seem tiny."

"Who'll play Captain Hook?" Gold asked.

"Sylvester Stallone. There will be a great sword fight on board his ship. He slaughters eighty people before Peter cuts off his head."

"I assume," said Dorothy, "there will be plenty of passionate love scenes."

"Yes indeed. Audiences insist on them. We'll make sure the musical is R-rated. It's the only way to get people away from their boob tubes and into a theater. I'm turning Peter into a teenage lesbian who likes to pretend she's a boy. Madonna will be dancing seminude while she sings. No point in concealing that beautiful body of hers."

"I once had a splendid meat body," said the tin man, "but now I can't say I miss it. There are advantages, you know, in being made of metal. If I were flesh and blood I'd be dead now from Bugsy's bullets, or drowned at the bottom of the sea after your thugs threw me over the side of your yacht."

"I have no idea what you're raving about," snarled Boggs. "You were never on my yacht."

"I was always made of straw," said the Scarecrow, "and a good thing, too. Otherwise I'd have been smashed to death when your hired killers threw me off the Empire State Building."

"Shut up!" snapped Boggs. "You're talking garbage."

"Calm down, Buffalo," said Sammy. "I'd like to know more about your musical. If Peter Pan is to be a female, how will you handle the role of Wendy?"

"We're turning Wendy into an elderly man who likes to talk nonstop. I expect to sign up Mickey Rooney for the part."

"You can't call him Wendy. What will his name be?"

"It's Windy."

"On the contrary," said the Scarecrow. "This morning not a single breeze was blowing."

Dorothy gave the straw man a kick on his shin. Of course he couldn't feel any pain, but he knew his leg had been kicked. "I couldn't resist it," he whispered to Dorothy.

"Tell me about the music for your Peter Pan," said Gold. "Have you found a composer?"

"We're negotiating with Andrew Lloyd Webber, though we may not be able to meet his fee. He's very high priced, you know. John Updike has agreed to write the lyrics."

"I must say I'm impressed."

"Thank you. Now how about telling *me* some of *your* plans for *The Emerald City of Oz*."

"Fair enough, Buffalo. I'll let you in on a little secret I haven't yet told the media. I've changed my mind about basing my film on Baum's book. It has a wonderful crazy plot about an invasion of Oz that actually happened back in 1910, but now I have an even more exciting story to tell. I've hired a writer and lifelong Oz fan named Martin Gardner to write a true account of the recent adventures of Dorothy and her friends. Before they left Oz to come here they visited several remarkable villages in the Gillikin country. That will make for some great movie scenes. And they've had many unusual experiences in the United States, thanks mainly to you."

"What do you mean, thanks to me?" Buffalo snorted angrily. "I never set eyes on Miss Gale and her two freaks until now."

Gold ignored the remark. "I plan to base my musical on Gardner's manuscript. Of course he can't finish it until my guests are safely back in Oz.

"You amaze me, Sambo," Boggs replied in a scornful tone.

"You still won't admit that these three sitting here are imposters. Pray tell me, Sam, how are you going to explain in your film how they got here from Oz? Did Ozma teleport them here with her ridiculous Magic Belt? And will she be waving that silly wand of hers to bring them back home?"

"I know you can't believe it," said Gold. "I can't blame you because nobody else can believe it either. But they're not imposters. They came here from Oz by way of a mysterious mathematical object called a Klein Bottle. It's a complicated story."

"You mean it's a *tall* story," snickered Boggs. "As I said before, you must think I'm awfully stupid to fall for such crap. I read some Oz books when I was a boy. I never much cared for them. I liked the Tom Swift books better. Baum was a lousy writer. I tried to read some of the Oz books by other writers but they were even worse. MGM's *Wizard* was a big success, but only because of Judy's great acting and singing. Today's audiences won't go to a movie unless they can expect to see lots of violence, bare flesh, splattered blood—"

"And car chases," Sammy interrupted.

"You got it. They love car chases that last for ten minutes and end with a car going over a cliff and exploding in a big burst of flame."

At the word *burst,* Boggs banged his fist on the table with such force that it overturned the vase of flowers.

Dorothy mopped up as much of the spill as she could with her cloth napkin. "How can there be car crashes in your film? When I was little my uncle took me to a silent movie about Peter Pan. I still remember how I clapped and clapped to save Tinkerbell. But I can't recall any cars in Neverland."

"You're right, young lady. "I'll be changing all that. Sambo here may prefer to stick to the old rural Oz described by Baum, but I'm turning Neverland into a modern industrial city with tall buildings and cars and airplanes."

"Sounds like quite a movie, Buffalo," said Gold as he lifted his glass and rattled its ice cubes. "It's only water, Buffalo, but let's have a toast to the success of Peter Pan."

"I'll drink to that," said Boggs, "although I much prefer whisky." He raised his glass and clanged it against Gold's so hard that the two glasses almost shattered.

The salty herring had done its job. Buffalo was extremely thirsty. He put the glass of water to his lips, leaned back his head, and in a few big gulps he drained the glass.

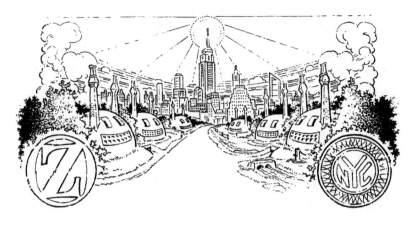

24

~cw~

BOGGS'S PUNISHMENT

BUFFALO ODERSBY Boggs dabbed his mustache with a corner of his napkin, then looked around the room with wide open eyes and a mystified frown. "Peter Pan? Who's Peter Pan?"

He glanced at the Scarecrow and Tin Woodman and was so startled that he dropped his napkin on the floor.

"Who are these crazy-looking creatures?" he shouted, as he slapped a palm on top of his bald head. "You look exactly like a scarecrow," he said, pointing a spoon toward the straw man. "And you," he added, turning toward the Tin Woodman, "you look like you're made of shiny steel! Can you talk?"

"I can," replied the tin man. "But I'm not made of steel.

I'm made of high quality nickel-plated tin. I polish it every morning after I oil my joints."

The Tin Woodman opened the door in his chest. From his hollow interior he took a large white jar that had been held by two clamps just below his heart. He held up the jar.

"I always carry this polish with me." He replaced the jar and closed the door, while Boggs almost tumbled off his chair.

Boggs scratched his chest and muttered to himself for several minutes before he regained enough composure to turn and glare at Gold and Dorothy. "And who are you? Who am I? *Where* am I?"

He glanced around the dining room with an expression that mixed bewilderment and terror. "I'm scared. I want to go home to Mommy and Daddy!"

The others at the table grinned at each other, raised their thumbs, and slapped one another's palms.

Gold had arranged for two nurses to be on hand. To signal them he tinkled a bell beside his plate. They entered the room from the kitchen, where they had been waiting, to lead Boggs to an ambulance parked on the street. He was taken to a Los Angeles psychiatric hospital.

In *The Magic of Oz* the Royal Historian tells how the mysterious word *PYRZQXGL*, if correctly pronounced, enables the speaker to transform anyone into any kind of animal.*

While Dorothy and Sammy were finishing their lunch, the

---

* Although I was never able to learn the correct pronunciation of this powerful magic word, I did notice the curious symmetrical structure of its letters. The curved lines on the word, as shown below, indicate the interweaving of the sequences PQR and XYZ. I assume that GL at the end stands for Glinda.

PYRZQXGL

Scarecrow mentioned the word, though without pronouncing it. "If I could only remember how to say it, I'd turn Buffalo into a cockroach and step on him."

The Tin Woodman shook his head. "That's because you don't have a heart, Scarecrow. I doubt very much if that word would work outside Oz. Even if it did, what you suggest would be much too cruel a fate for any person, even someone as wicked as Boggs."

"You forget," said Gold, "that Dorothy once used Ozma's Magic Belt to turn Ugu, the evil shoemaker who kidnapped Ozma, into a dove."

"I remember it well," said Dorothy. "As Baum recorded it in *The Lost Princess of Oz*, Ugu repented of his crimes. We all forgave him. I offered to turn him back into a man but he refused. He begged me to let him remain a contented and peaceful dove."

"A dove is much better than a cockroach," said the tin man. "Besides, Ugu was allowed to live. I'm glad, Scarecrow, you thought of the Forbidden Fountain."

Boggs had ruled his film empire with an iron hand. During his confinement to the mental hospital, where he was treated for amnesia, the executives who worked for him began squabbling and fighting for control of the company. Before the end of the year Boggs Pictures was in shambles. Gold was able to buy the studio and all its assets for a paltry fifty million. His first act as the new owner was to cancel plans for a Peter Pan musical.

Buffalo never regained any memories of his life beyond the age of ten. After three years in the hospital he recovered enough to be released in the custody of his sister, Mrs. Ima Crabbe. A Chicago resident, she agreed to let him live in her home and to take care of him. I'm told he is working as a street photographer inside Chicago's Loop. Using a Polaroid camera, he snaps color photos of pedestrians, then sells them for two dollars each.

Ima's young daughters Ura and Ada, and their little brother Hermit, are very fond of their kind simpleminded uncle. And Mrs. Crabbe makes sure he keeps himself clean and showers every other night.

When this information appeared in Glinda's Magic Book of Records, and was reprinted in *The Emerald City Times,* Professor Wogglebug sent the newspaper the following Limerick:

> *The socks worn by Buffalo Boggs*
> *Once smelled like a pen full of hogs.*
> > *But now he's so neat*
> > *That he washes his feet*
> *Every night when he takes off his togs.*

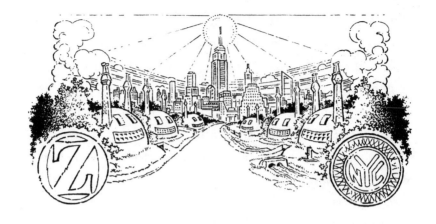

25

———✦✦✦———

H O M E

AFTER THE forbidden water had washed away Boggs's memories, Dorothy and her friends remained in the United States for two more weeks to make a final tour of radio and television talk shows. In bookstores all over the land they autographed Oz books on sale as well as older editions brought to the store by Oz buffs.

Martin Gardner spent many weeks recording conversations with the three visitors and with Samuel Gold. Gardner's novel, *Visitors from Oz*, was published in 1998 by St. Martin's Press. Gold hoped to complete his Oz film by the end of the year 2000. That was the hundred-year anniversary of the publication of *The Wonderful Wizard of Oz* by the small Chicago firm of George M. Hill.

The Scarecrow and the tin man would have liked to stay in the United States a few weeks longer so they could see the Grand Canyon and visit Disneyland, but Dorothy was increasingly anxious to return to Oz.

Gold was sad to see them leave, but of course he was ecstatic about all the wonderful publicity they had generated for his musical. He persuaded Michael Patrick Hearn, author of the definitive biography of Baum, to serve as one of the film's consultants. The finest computer artists were hired to animate the Oz characters who were not flesh and blood. Gold did his best to persuade Dorothy to remain in California to star in his picture, but she refused.

"You know I can't sing or dance."

"It doesn't matter," Gold replied. "All you have to do is move your lips while someone else does the vocalizing. As for dancing, computer techniques are so powerful today that we can easily put your face on a dancer's body."

Dorothy shook her head vigorously. "I've had my fill of the United States. You know, Mr. Gold, I almost got killed several times. Besides, I'm terribly, terribly homesick. I can't wait to get back to the Emerald City."

The only way the visitors could return to Oz was by way of the Klein Bottle. Gold flew back with them to Manhattan, where they stayed in his apartment for several days to plan how to handle their return.

The portion of the bottle's large tube, where it twisted through the fourth dimension, still hung fifteen feet above the grass in Central Park, near the reservoir. Although it was invisible, the tube on either side of the portion that was open to our universe's space could be felt by anyone who knew it was there.

Gold owned a tall stepladder that could be used to reach the tube. It was decided that Dorothy and the Scarecrow would have little difficulty climbing up through the tube, but the tin man posed a serious problem. His metal hands and feet would surely be too slippery on the bottle's smooth interior to allow him to work his way upward. The plan was as follows.

Gold would send Glinda an E-mail letter, asking her to arrange with Ozma for the Sawhorse to return to Ballville with the Red Wagon and the Yellow Cart. He would bring along the braided tin rope that Ku-Klip had supplied and which they had used for fastening the bottle to the cart. Once Dorothy and the Scarecrow were through the bottle and on Gillikin ground, they would lower the rope into the bottle so the Tin Woodman could grasp it and be pulled up.

Four in the morning was chosen as the best time for the travelers to enter the bottle. Glinda and Ozma would determine the day, allowing the Sawhorse plenty of time to get to Ballville. The date would then be sent to Gold by E-mail.

There was much discussion about what to do with the Klein Bottle after it was no longer needed. The Scarecrow suggested it be given to Big Jim Foote.

"We thought the trash he dropped through it would fall on Central Park," said the straw man, "but that was a mistake. Big Jim's house is so far east of Ballville that his garbage would drop harmlessly into the North Atlantic as food for the seagulls."

Dorothy strongly objected. "The bottle's too dangerous to

leave with Big Jim or anyone else. We must either destroy it or let Ozma store it away in one of her palace's basements."

After all arrangements were made, and the return date set, Gold and his guests waited until it was two-thirty in the morning before they walked to the spot where the Klein Bottle was suspended. The Tin Woodman carried Gold's stepladder. The Scarecrow carried Dorothy's suitcase.

After the ladder was unfolded and in place, Dorothy agreed to go first. She had been fond of climbing trees when she was a small girl in Kansas, and was sure she would have no difficulty pulling herself upward through the mysterious tube.

She gave Sammy a bear hug and a kiss on the cheek. "Thank you for inviting us here," she said, her blue eyes moist. "It was a wonderful adventure for all of us. I hope your picture's a big success."

"How could it not be, Dorothy, thanks to you and your friends. I'm sorry you won't stay to act in my musical, but I understand how you feel. I hope, though, you'll visit us again sometime. You know you'll always be welcome to stay in my New York apartment."

"Thank you again, Mr. Gold. I may take you up on that someday, but it won't be for a long time."

"Do you suppose Glinda and Ozma would let me visit Oz before I'm too old?"

"Perhaps. I promise I'll speak to them about it. We may keep the Klein Bottle in case it's needed again."

The night was warm and cloudy, without a star in the sky except for one bright star that was probably a planet. The buzzing of cicadas made it hard to hear the traffic that never stops rolling on nearby Fifth Avenue.

Gold had brought with him a large flashlight. He aimed its beam at Dorothy while she climbed the stepladder.

It took Dorothy several minutes, waving her hands, to locate the part of the tube that twisted through the fourth dimension. She climbed back down so the Tin Woodman could move the ladder several feet to bring it directly under the tube's open section.

Dorothy had no difficulty lifting herself into the tube and crawling upward by pressing her hands firmly against the tube's smooth sides. At the top, she vaulted over the bottle's rim into the bright sunshine of Oz. She took deep breaths of the fragrant Gillikin air.

"It smells so much better here," she said aloud, "than in New York."

"Hello, Dorothy," the Sawhorse called out. He had been waiting patiently beside the waterfall for several hours. "Welcome home! Ozma told me about some of your adventures down under, but only the few she happened to catch on her Magic Picture. You'll have to tell me more and fill in the details."

"I'll be happy to, Sawhorse, on our ride to the Emerald City. We had some narrow escapes. But for now we must get my friends up through the bottle."

No sooner had she said this than they saw the straw man's padded fingers on the side of the bottle's rim, and heard him sing out "Tol-de-ri-de-oh!" No one, not even the Scarecrow, knew what this meant, but he liked to sing it whenever he was especially happy.

"It was easier than I expected," he remarked as he climbed out of the bottle and got to his feet beside Dorothy. "Now we must get the rope down to my old friend."

The Scarecrow tied one end of the braided tin rope to the back of the Yellow Cart. The other end was lowered into the bottle until it was down far enough for the Tin Woodman to grasp.

"I'm ready!" they heard him yell through the bottle's opening.

The Sawhorse pulled the Red Wagon. It pulled the Yellow Cart, which in turn pulled the tin man upward. They could hear his body clanking against the bottle's sides. When he reached the rim, Dorothy and the Scarecrow helped him climb out. He had carried his axe in one hand and Dorothy's suitcase in the other. He put both on the ground so he could straighten his funnel hat which had gotten tipped to one side.

"I think my axe blade and the tip of my nose made some scratches on the tube," he said, "but I don't think it damaged the bottle much. It's great to be back in Oz."

In Central Park, Samuel Gold wiped away some tears as he folded the stepladder to carry it back to his apartment.

The shovels were still under the bushes where the travelers had concealed them, and Dorothy's sleeping bag was on the ground nearby. It took almost an hour for the two men to dig up the Klein Bottle and fill the hole with the large pile of dirt at the hole's side. The two of them, with Dorothy's help, managed to lift the huge bottle onto the Yellow Cart and fasten it down with the rope. The Scarecrow put Dorothy's suitcase and sleeping bag in the back of the Red Wagon.

For breakfast Dorothy ate some of the purple berries that grew by the waterfall. The Tin Woodman brought her several drinks of the waterfall's apple cider.

The travelers were unanimous in not wanting to revisit Ballville or to stop at Wonderland or Mount Olympus on their ride back to the Emerald City. During the ride, Dorothy told the Sawhorse some of the events that happened to them on their visit to the United States. He listened with intense interest, occasionally rolling his knotty eyes upward and interjecting wry comments that had them all laughing.

Ozma invited Uncle Henry and Aunt Em to be present in the Royal Palace when the travelers arrived. Dorothy hugged and kissed her aunt and uncle, then turned to embrace Ozma. She picked up Toto who had been looking up at her and wagging his tail.

"I missed you," the little dog remarked after he licked Dorothy's cheek.

"Did you bring me anything?" Eureka asked. She had curled up on top of Dorothy's sleeping bag.

"And oh, Aunt Em!" Dorothy exclaimed with a choke in her voice, "I'm so glad to be home again!"

Ozma took Dorothy's advice about the Klein Bottle. She ordered that it be preserved in a locked room on the lowest of her palace's three basements. It might just be useful, she said, some time in the future.

Glinda spent several days going carefully through her vast library of books on sorcery until she found an unusual way to bring Zoroaster back from the Atlantic to his family in the Nonestic Ocean. But that's a long story. Maybe I can tell it some day if I write another Oz book.

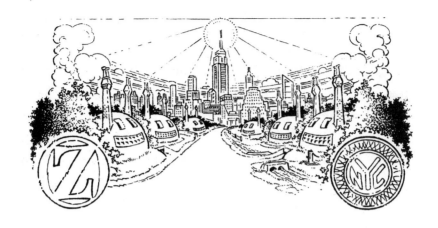

ABOUT THE AUTHOR

MARTIN GARDNER is a self-taught mathematician who is best known for the thirty years during which he wrote *Scientific American*'s column on recreational mathematics—columns now collected in fifteen volumes. In addition, he has written some fifty other books about science, philosophy, literature, and conjuring. The most popular of his books have been *The Annotated Alice* and *The Night Is Large*, a selection of essays. He is also the author of a novel, *The Flight of Peter Fromm*, and *The No-Sided Professor*, a collection of short stories.

Like the Samuel Gold of his Oz book, Gardner learned to read by looking over his mother's shoulder while she read aloud from *The Wizard of Oz*. Before he started high school in Tulsa, where he was born in 1914, he had zipped through and loved all of Baum's other Oz books and non-Oz fantasies.

The first detailed account of Baum's life was Gardner's "The Royal Historian of Oz," a two-part essay that ran in *Fantasy and Science Fiction* magazine. He has since written introductions to six paperback facsimile editions of Baum fantasies. He was a founder of The International Wizard of Oz Club and the recipient of its second annual honorary medal. He continues to contribute to the club's handsome quarterly, *The Baum Bugle*.

"There still are, I'm sorry to say," Gardner recently remarked, "a few gray-brained librarians, psychologists, and critics of juvenile literature who actually believe that fantasies like the Oz books are harmful for children. It's a curious opinion that Gilbert Chesterton considered close to mortal sin."

Gardner is fond of quoting the following passage from Chesterton's essay "The Dragon's Grandmother," a stirring defense of fairy tales:

> Folk-lore means that the soul is sane, but that the universe is wild and full of marvels. Realism means that the world is dull and full of routine, but that the soul is sick and screaming. The problem of the fairy tale is—what will a healthy man do with a fantastic world? The problem of the modern novel is—what will a madman do with a dull world? In the fairy tales the cosmos goes mad; but the hero does not go mad. In the modern novels the hero is mad before the book begins, and suffers from the harsh steadiness and cruel sanity of the cosmos.

Mr. Gardner has been given numerous awards for his writings about science and math, as well as two honorary doctorates. Before beginning his association with *Scientific American* he was, for eight years, contributing editor of *Humpty Dumpty's Magazine*. He provided a story and a poem for each issue, and designed all the magazine's activity features. For the past sixteen years he has lived quietly with his wife, Charlotte, in the western mountains of North Carolina.